Enjoy ~ oper of sto

Marianne Paul

TENDING MEMORY

Marianne Paul

Marianne Paul (signature)

BookLand press

TORONTO, CANADA

Published by:
Bookland Press Inc.
6021 Yonge Street
Suite 1010
Toronto, Ontario M2M 3W2
Canada
www.booklandpress.com

Printed and bound in Canada.

Library and Archives Canada Cataloguing in Publication

Paul, Marianne, 1955-
    Tending memory / Marianne Paul.

ISBN 978-0-9780838-5-4

    I. Title.

PS8581.A829146 2007   C813'.54   C2007-901171-3

For my mother,
Marjorie Golden,
with immense love

"Figure it out if you can. Pick the truth from the untruth like crows picking clean the bones of a lesser bird. Swallow the story and leave only the lie, sun-bleached and bone-dry."

~ *Michaela*

"Gypsies lie. They lie a lot – more often and more inventively than other people... On the whole, lying is a cheerful affair. Embellishments are intended to give pleasure."

~ *Isabel Fonseca*
Bury Me Standing. The Gypsies and Their Journey

PART ONE

The Start of Story

Chapter 1

Your hands are deft and the peel is thin. You slice into the apple, feed me the pieces, even the bruise, your fingers to my mouth. I lick your skin and taste the salt. It seems the men in my life are moved to feed me.

I laugh, and you ask what is funny.

I tell you about Thomas.

Start with the leaving.

It is as good a place as any to tend memory.

Chapter 2

Thomas turns, shifts position.

He mutters words, protesting a bad dream. I hold my breath, think about slipping into bed to appease him, to move him back into sleep, but don't. It would only arouse him. The slightest touch does that to Thomas.

I open drawers quietly, remove socks and underwear, roll the socks into balls, pull on the underwear, two pairs, one over the other - what you carry on your body, less to carry on your back. Search the floor for tossed clothing, some mine, some not, it doesn't matter. Take a flannel shirt in my hands, push it into my face. Smell the scent, sweat and after-shave and cigarette smoke, linger in it. The scent is as close as I will get to a home.

I feel a moment of sadness at my leaving, a nostalgia for Thomas. It passes, and I keep his flannel shirt as a memento, roll it up, pack it.

This is a trick I've learned, rolling clothes in a tight log, stacking them like a woodpile into the bag. Efficient packing is an art. So is efficient leaving. Dawn is best. Get out before the rest of the world knows what you're doing. No tears, no angry words, no begging that you stay.

Then I shut the door behind me, tiptoe down the creaking stairs past the other rooms, different stories snoring behind each door, step out on the street. The sky is the colour of elephant skin.

I walk to the highway at the edge of town. You know the highway that I mean, it is always there, no matter the dot on the map. The road that takes you right into town, as if it can't wait for you to arrive, and then takes you right out of town, as if it can't wait for you to leave.

*****

A BMW. I think I've hit pay dirt, stick out a thumb. The car whizzes by, spitting stones at me. I give the driver the finger.

A trucker blasts his horn at the gesture. He doesn't stop either, sends more stones flying. So I hitch up my skirt, stick out a leg, dare the bastards to follow the line wherever their imaginations lead. Frilly lace panties, black garter belt, butt-splitting thongs, or no underwear at all. None will imagine the truth. That I wear men's jockey shorts, faded blue, needing a wash, and "borrowed" from Thomas. Imagination is such a liar, but no one really cares, particularly not the trucker who screeches to a halt at the shoulder of the road, kicking up dust like a cowboy.

I haul myself into the rig. The cowboy doesn't say much, just keeps grinning as if he's roped the calf. The grey sky gives way to rose-pink, and I imagine it is the colour of the inside of the elephant's ear. If you lift up the flap, take a peek, you'd see rose-pink.

We weave in and out of the traffic thickening with day. From the cab, even the limousines look inconsequential. The cowboy cuts a path finger-width-close to a bitch in a Fiat convertible, her hair blowing in the wind. She looks up at us. Fear flashes across her model face, and I hoot as we leave her behind.

At high noon we pull off the highway into a service station. It snakes with people. I itch for coffee, stand at the tail end of one such snake. The cowboy has gone to piss. I feel like a viper, spit words at the woman in line ahead of me. She jumps at my hissing. I feel impatience in my body, shift foot to foot to foot. Waiting in line is like staying in one town too long.

Then it happens - like being stoned, but I'm clean.

Something flutters from my hand.

Softly, as if caught in a current, like a bird catches air beneath its wings. Like the wind lifts the fluff of a dandelion seed. Time moves differently, and I'm inside the difference. The moment is slow. Clear. Like cold air.

I act, without thinking. Reach for the object.

But object is a flawed word - it implies weight.

This thing has no weight. It flutters like a feather from a hummingbird's breast.

Then the moment shifts.

Clarity is gone, and the air is hot. Legs close around me, and the snake uncoils. Time speeds up.

I grasp the object in my fingers just before it touches the floor, look at it. A dime.

A fluttering dime. How can that be?

Chapter 3

Doubting Thomas, now there's a man of admirable skepticism. *Show me the wounds*, the Apostle said to the others as they whispered ghost tales around the campfire, roasted fish on olive branches, rolled the rush of events in Jerusalem about their heads and their tongues, trying to shape it into truth, what to believe.

Doubting Thomas didn't weep hosannas, fall to his knees at the sight of Jesus's burial cloths strewn across the empty tomb like the after-effects of a drunken party.

Show me the wounds, he said.

Give me a man like that, and if I had my choice of apostle as lover, I'd take Thomas. Kiss his brow, wash the dirt of the road from his feet with fine oil, dry his feet with my hair. Thomas, a man who needs to put his fingers in the wounds, feel the gaping holes, still wet and warm and raw.

But I didn't get the Apostle.

I got the Aquinas.

I met this other Thomas, my Aquinas, at a seminary. I had sneaked into the library looking for a place to sleep, and not wanting to work for it. I'd done that before, searched out the library in a university town. University libraries are open late and camouflage me well. I can look bleary-eyed, blood-shot and overdosed. I can play student, sleep at a table, book as a pillow, pages spread open, cushioning my head. I can fake academia, scholastic orgasm, words like kisses, talk passionately of philosophy, theology, history, literature. That was Thomas's downfall. Confused body for mind. Mistook ideas spoken with passion for love.

Sleeping in a library. It's one of those tricks extracted from experience and learned from need. A travel tip you won't get in the glossy travel books that line the shelves of the fancy bookstores, expensive books like high-priced call girls, slick and glamorous to the eye, books to seduce armchair travellers. I am not an armchair traveller.

Then there are those other books, drab and cheap. *See the world on a shoestring budget.* They extol the virtues of hostels. Neither am I virtuous. I abhor hostels, they remind me of shelters. Rows of mattresses lined up on the floor like brave, sick soldiers too long in the trenches.

I don't want to spend my nights with drifting people, the sense of a ship that is listing, nothing to power it, the engines shutting down. The shelters are like that, full of people who've shut down. I see in it their eyes, dull and resigned, no travel left in them. They shove their belongings in shopping bags and leave in the morning, shelter rules, out by nine. They circle the streets, check the garbage dumpsters, claim the heating vents, beg at the corners. They out-wait time until the shelter opens again. Me, when I pack my bags and leave in the morning, I leave for good, don't travel that way again.

So I'll sleep in a library, but never a hostel, never in a shelter. Never in a church, either, but not for the reasons you might think. Church doors are dead-bolted at night; modern salvation is nine-to-five.

When I was a little girl, the church doors were always unlocked, left open to snare back the prodigal sons and daughters who couldn't sleep with their sins.

As a child, I'd run away to the church at night.

Curl up in the pulpit like the barn cat in the loft, and when the cat was restless and had to roam, crawl under the communion rail into the space where only the priests and God were allowed to go. Paw the contents of secret drawers, stroke the gold and purple vestments, sip the blood left in the bottom of the chalice, the silver metal cold upon my lips. Eat communion wafers like potato chips, light the altar candles, tall and white and elegant. Lie back and stare up at the stained glass windows, the flickering flame casting long shadows against the darkness.

Chapter 4

My mother and I lived alone in an old house where the wind blew through spaces in the clapboard, where we put blankets against the cracks at the bottom of the door so that the snow did not blow in like sand through a desert.

My father left when I was two, and a jolly good thing too, we thought, watching his back disappear across the yard and into the world. *He's a no-good bum, good for nothing and hard on food*, my mother would say, her words matching the rhythm of the chair, words like swells rocking a ship.

This night, like every evening, my mother sat in the rocking chair and started into routine, pushing her legs against the hardwood floor, setting the chair in motion. Back and forth, back and forth, the rockers rubbed rhythmically against the floor.

I sat on the floor beside her, the rockers cutting dangerously close to my fingers, my giant box of Crayola in front of me. I drew pictures on scraps of paper, and listened to the rockers against the hardwood floor. Felt awe at the concept of possibility, and chose colour as if performing a sacrament.

Sun slipped through the window and lit a pathway. Dust particles floated around me, and I mistook their weightlessness for timelessness, but the latter was an illusion.

Grey crept upon the room, marking the passage of the day, the passage of light to shadows. The rockers, too, measured the progress of time, kept step with the journey of afternoon into dusk into night. Then the rocking lost strength, like an ebbing tide, until I sat in blackness, and silence, and stillness, and nothing was ever the same again.

I crawled up into my mother's lap for protection from the shadows, and tried to rock the chair. Pushed with all my might against her body, pushed my tiny legs against her thighs, wanting to make her legs press the hardwood floor, to set the rockers marking time again. Finally, I gave up. Curled in her lap, put my head against her breast.

The room grew cold. I slid off her lap, pulled the quilt from her bed. Climbed back up into my mother, wrapped the quilt around both of us as best I could, and watched morning return through the window.

Her body felt like autumn settling into winter, how ice forms at the edge of a pond, small pockets of air trapped and jiggling, water still swirling underneath until it too finally hardens.

The ice crept into her veins, crept into her limbs, and her fingers grew cold and stiff. I rubbed her hands, as if trying to ignite a fire through friction, but it didn't help. She didn't stir.

So I let her rest. Once or twice, I reached for her face, stroking her as she had stroked me. I imagine it well, my mother stroking my cheek, my mouth opening instinctively, moving towards touch like a baby bird. The same way I stroke your face now, while telling you this story. Trace cheekbone to lips, your tongue instinctively reaching for me, mouth closing on my finger.

I did not like the dark, did not then, do not now. Avoid darkness by lighting candles, setting them a-twinkle around me like so many stars. I hear the sea at night is like that, like a darkened room full of a trillion candles.

When I was a child, I pretended I was on the deck of a ship, falling up and down with the waves, candle-stars poking light into the night and reflected in the bottomless waters. I plan to make it there, yet, to the sea. Have set out a trillion times, once for each star in the sky.

    I will never leave you, my mother had said as I watched my father's back disappear, watched him turn into a single black dot of ink against the flat pen line of the horizon. And I believed her. Felt her hand engulf mine, as warm as truth.

Chapter 5

Whispers and pitying looks and wagging heads and thick perfumes. Brief touches and fancy cakes and heavy casseroles and endless tea. I didn't cry, not then, not in their parlours. Not even later, in their darkened bedrooms piled high with needlepoint pillows, and brocade bedcovers, and thick drapes that kept out the sun.

They mistook my lack of tears as a lack of understanding, a stupid child, they thought, or perhaps that I was simply too young. It allowed them to speak about what had happened more loudly, more boldly, and with a perverse delight, having eluded death so far themselves.

It's a blessing she doesn't know the truth, a woman named Mildred spoke to everyone, and to no one in particular, as if truth mattered. *Poor child, asleep on the lap, must have been there for hours.*

Mildred heaped scalloped potatoes onto a plastic plate, covering the mound with a slice of ham, then sat in a parlour chair, balancing the plate on her stocking-ed knees. I watched the plate teeter, fascinated by the scientific logic behind the action. If she dug food from one side of the plate, disrupted the equilibrium, the balance, then the other side, now being heavier, would go down.

She was an adventurer of sorts, I decided, in awe with the way she pushed fate, no order to the locations from which she spooned her food, the plate rolling up and down, back and forth, like a ship caught in crosswinds.

I crawled over and sat at her feet, straightened up and stretched my back so that I was eye-level with her knees. Watched intently, predicting the dipping of the plate in response to her hand movement.

Mildred ignored me.

Death was sudden, she said, spooning, chewing, talking, swallowing. *Heart just stopped dead in its tracks. Strong one moment, bang, then nothing.*

I wanted to tell her it wasn't true. It didn't happen that way. There was no track. Just my mother and me and the rocking chair and the lessening sun. Her heart didn't stop suddenly, beating strong and then nothing. Life slid out of her. Slowly, calmly, so you wouldn't even know the point of the stopping.

I tried to set the record straight. Tried to tell Mildred that I had been there, head pressed into my mother's chest. Heard her heartbeat, fading in that way that sound dwindles, until you're not quite sure you still hear it, a frequency just beyond grasp, until that too fades away.

I reached for Mildred's hem, held a piece in my hand, tugged on it in the way I would tug on my mother's skirts, long and flowing about her ankles.

Mildred looked at me in horror, and then lunged for her plate. If she only hadn't lunged, the plate would have stayed upright, but she did lunge. Potatoes and pig tumbled onto her skirt, down her stockings, into her shoes, and scattered across the rug that had come in a boat all the way from Persia. Mildred leapt to her feet, loomed over me as tall as a crows-nest, face bright red.

In the mayhem, "they" grabbed me by the hands and pulled me away so that I flew like a kite, legs flapping in the air. Put me to bed in a shadowed room and locked the door behind them, the sound of their footsteps receding like my mother's heartbeats.

My eyes grew accustomed to the shadows and I kicked away the blankets. Sat at the edge of the mattress, dangling my legs over the side, and then pushed off. Ran away for the first time that night. Ran across the long dark room and hid behind the drapes. Peered out the window at the stars until they faded into the day, and then I curled up on the floor and slept.

Chapter 6

The seminary library is a neatly ordered labyrinth, like the minds of the men who frequent it, their own private brothel, touching the pages like fingers on skin. There's a reverence in the act, and I envy the pages. The men who have touched me had hunger in their fingers, but seldom awe.

Thousands of books stretch in rows from floor to ceiling. I wonder if each has been pressed opened and read. It seems an impossible task, all these books, but the spines are old and used.

I settle into the armchair, slouching low, one leg slung over the side like a fish line. Dangling is good for pretending you're someone else. I dangle my leg over the armchair, and rock my foot. The action says I'm comfortable. This is my place. I belong here, in this chair, in this library.

My body is hidden in baggy sweatshirt and pants. I wear a Nike baseball cap, pull the hood of the sweatshirt over my head so that my shadow looks like a cobra, my face shielded. The visor of the baseball cap is black suede leather and perfectly curved. Old men wear baseball caps with visors flat and wide. The seminary students take no notice of me. They think I'm one of them. A wannabe theologian, but more than that, one with a set of balls. I'm tall for a woman, but average height for a man. My frame is slight, my breasts and hips small, my yellow hair cropped short in tufts. Lying about gender is easy for me.

I remember the tiny hoops down the cartilage of my ear and remove them one by one, leaving only the stud in the earlobe. Shove the hoops into the pouch of my knapsack. Earrings or not, the seminary students pay me no notice. They're too busy with their books. It's a good thing. It rains outside like Noah's flood, Gilgamesh's too, and I need a dry place to sleep, having no ark to call my own.

I use a book as a foil. Read. Watch the others. Map out comings and goings, look for weaknesses to exploit. Read some more. *Early Church Fathers.* What else have I to do, but read? Grow hungry, that's what. I'm hungry now. I haven't eaten since morning.

A seminary student studies in the carrel against the wall. He's older than me, but not by much. He's nondescript really, and not worth noticing, except for the cream-cheese bagel and sesame seed crackers that sit in front of him like ornaments rather than food. He unwraps the bagel. Spreads out the Saran wrap, neatly flattens it like a tablecloth, smoothes out the wrinkles, and sits the bagel on top. Continues to read. An hour later, the bagel still sits there, intact, not a bite taken out of it. The crackers, too. Ignored for book. He fancies himself an ascetic. The Saint of the Uneaten Bagel. I scoff. I'm not one for self-denial.

I read about ascetics while passing the time in the library. Lurid crazy saintly stuff, *National Inquirer* stuff, cut-off-the-penis-to-deny-the-body-and-save-the-soul stuff.

First let me tell you about Origen, second century church philosopher. Aspiring to be neither male nor female, but androgynous and redeemed. He starved himself, wouldn't eat the bagel, either. Slept alone. Naked body on naked ground. Martyrdom and celibacy are good for the soul, he said, feet bloodied and shoe-less. Death to the body is redemption, Origen added, and then castrated himself.

Then there is Jerome, *Saint* Jerome at that. Saint is such a gentle word, like a breeze brushing by your ear, or a soft wind slipping through an open window. You trust the word, both the sound and the connotation, what you hear and what it means. They name schools for Saint Jerome, named this library after him, can you believe that? If we knew our namesakes better, we'd be more careful with the naming. Knew their human narrative, how their story unfolded, the truth about them, as clearly as we know the lie.

But the saddest story in the seminary books is that of Lady Blaesilla. Faint and fragile, she slipped away like an echo. You've never heard of her before, am I right? How can one speak of Saint Jerome without whispering Lady Blaesilla's name, wrapping her name around his for all history, like snakes entwined? But she is forgotten, no libraries named for her.

I can't imagine giving myself so completely to a man as Lady Blaesilla gave herself to Jerome. She followed him into the desert. Saint Jerome, the wild man, whispering passionate seductions into her ear, *body is nothing, tame it, starve it, deny it, stay with me, and find paradise.* A common act of ascetics, it seems, to seek the desert, as if scorching sun and sand can leave a cinder where there is fire, can burn away the flesh and leave only the bones.

Did St. Jerome see Lady Blaesilla among the dancing girls that tormented his dreams throughout his life, desire for the flesh un-exorcised? And if Lady Blaesilla danced for him, was she young and full like the day they had met? Or did she come into his dreams as the day she had died? Unwashed and neglected, body wasted and old, although barely a woman, no older than me.

Chapter 7

"Me-chaela, Me-e-chael-aaa."

I awoke to their calling me. My name sounded strange and unfamiliar from their mouths, as if it were not mine, but belonged to another. And so I imagined another Michaela, a child who looked like me, ugly and small in stature, with no sense of physical substance. Hair like mine, the tassel of corn, skin paler than the moon, eyes washed out and tinged blue.

Another Michaela to take my place so that I could stay here, behind the drapes, while *she* answered their calls, said the words that pleased them, sat unwavering in chairs that did not rock, stood ground in a way that I could never.

I began to sway, just slightly, so not to set the curtain rippling.

"Me-chaela, Me-e-chael-aaa." They rustled the blankets. Peeled away the bed covers as if peeling a banana, as if they'd find me there beneath the skin.

Voices grew agitated, and other voices joined them.

"Look under the bed," said one, the thud of knees and hands against the floor. No Me-chaela under the bed, someone else chanted, the words like a nursery rhyme.

"Try the closet," said another.

The sound of my name receded into the cavern of the closet. "Me-chaela, Me-e-chael-aaa" – but they did not find me. I pushed my forehead into my knees, clasped my legs, rocked faster on my heels.

"Do you think she ran away?"

Now the voice was close.

I stopped rocking, made myself grow smaller.

"She couldn't have left the room - unless she slipped through the keyhole," one of them said.

"Keyhole or not, she's gone," a voice snapped, and I recognized Mildred. "So she's run away, is that surprising? It's bred into her genes."

They left the room, searched for hours in other places, as if I *could* slip through keyholes. Could very well be hiding with the cutlery in the kitchen drawer, behind the jars in the pantry, under the potatoes in the potato bin, stacked on my side with the bottles in the wine cellar. Furniture scraped across the floor, sofas and chairs and tables pulled out from the wall and then back into place, doors and drawers opened and shut, no Michaela in the corners, no Michaela under the rug, no Michaela standing in the hallway with the canes and umbrellas.

I peered over the windowsill.

The men searched the grounds, a manly thing to do. Unlike the women who turned the house upside down with the vigour of a good cleaning, the men conducted themselves with the grim resignation of finding a body. They shone flashlights into tiny crawl spaces where only a child could fit, examined the compost heap and then the ditch along the road, spread apart the elephant-ear leaves along the fence, dredged the pond.

Finally, I grew sleepy, left my hiding place behind the curtain and crawled back into bed.

"Holy Mother of Jesus!" Mildred yelled.

I awoke to Mildred crossing herself, clutching the key to my room as if it were a crucifix to protect her. And if not protection, then undeniable proof that she had searched this room, and had locked this door, and I could not possibly be here.

Magic. Black magic. Evil-eye, gypsy curse magic. Mildred whispered it to the others, who whispered it to *their* others, and so story grew, twisted its way through telling and re-telling.

Chapter 8

The Saint of the Uneaten Bagel - I size him up. Figure I can take him. He's scrawny. It's obvious he doesn't pump iron. Doesn't dig ditches. Doesn't work long hours in a warehouse packing heavy boxes. His mother probably pays his tuition, no need for him to work. I imagine his hands, white and soft. He's a reader, an avid page-turner. His reflexes will be slow from lack of use. Lack of the physical. I calculate the time it would take to make the snatch, grab the bagel, sprint through the door and race down the two flights to the street. By the time my action registers in his body as reaction, I'll be long gone and the bagel too. And so what if he catches me? I have fought bigger men and lived.

I place the book on the table, pages spread open and face-down. Stretch my arms, wiggle my back, roll my shoulders. My motions are nothing more than appearance. A staged lie, as if I only pause to stretch and then will return to my studies, chastened by the momentary weakness in my body. In reality, I watch for the almost-perfect moment to act. Almost perfect, and never perfect, for to wait for perfection is to wait forever. I won't wait forever.

But then the unexpected happens. The Saint stands up,

leaves, disappears into the maze of rows of book before I can snatch.

The bagel remains on the desk alongside his books, his coat slung invitingly over the back of the chair. I wait. Alert. Listening for a sound of what's to come. But no one comes. I grow bold, don't bother to hide my intentions, swagger to the carrel, check out his things.

A pen is laid casually across the notebook. A silver pen, probably a gift from the tuition-paying mother. The ink leaves blue watery waves across the clean white page, and I'm reminded of the ocean. The ocean-ink stops mid-sentence, as if a question has broken upon it like a cresting wave. No doubt, the Saint is off tracing a fact or a footnote, something obscure and useless and buried in minutia.

An ascetic doesn't understand the ocean. Tides pulling at the heart that you're powerless to deny. Now I understand tides, have greater right to the pen. I pocket it. Feel justified. Then I take the bagel, bite into it. Chew slowly. Savour the food. It's the savouring that gives greatest pleasure. The act of prolonging. I'm in paradise.

I steal the sesame-seed crackers, too. Put them in my knapsack for later pleasure. Consider taking the Saint's coat, but that will draw attention. I leave it behind, but not before slipping my hands into the pockets for cash. Nothing. It doesn't surprise me. What can you expect from an ascetic?

Chapter 9

Every spring and fall, like the certainty of the seasons themselves, Pear changed the outer windows. I much preferred the screens. Howled like a wolf each time he lugged out the long wooden ladder from the storage shed in the autumn. Raised it shakily upward, top end wobbling across my window, until the ladder rested with a thud against the grey-slate shingles that covered the house.

Leaned back my head and bayed like a young wolf at an imaginary moon with each step he climbed, callused hand over callused hand. Until finally, the white tuft of hair appeared over my windowsill, and we were face to face, his black sad eyes looking into mine.

And I howled some more - maybe at his sadness - long after he took down the screen and replaced it with the thick frosted winter glass. Long after he climbed down the ladder, thumped it a window to the right, and repeated the process. Circling the big house as if he circumnavigated the world.

But when spring came, I pulled at his pant leg, pulled at his shirt tail, pulled at his sweater sleeves. Wrapped my arms around his leg, wrapped my legs around his ankle, rode his knee, wouldn't let go, so that he had to drag me that way, one leg stiff with the extra weight, swinging as if he had a peg leg. "Pear, Pear, Pear," I cried. "The windows."

Even though the nights would still dip below zero, and one last storm sat at the edge of the winter, my desires would turn to the screen window, like the old ladies' thoughts would turn to spring cleaning, and I would pester Pear.

First in English, and when I realized he didn't understand my pleas, or at least, pretended not to understand my Anglais words, then I learned the French.

"Fenêtre, fenêtre, fenêtre, s'il vous plait," I'd cry, mimicking his Quebecois accent, standing on my tiptoes and pointing upward.

And finally my pestering would work.

Pear would unwind the old green hose with its pinholes and little geysers, turn on the faucet, aim a gushing stream of water through one side of the screen, then flip it over to the other. Wash away the dirt and brown crumbled leaf bits, the threads of spider webs, the dead flies, the cocoon moth pockets. Lean the screens to dry against the house, all in a row, like cemetery stones.

In concert, the Aunties aired my bedroom. Stripped the bed of the flannelette sheets, the winter wool blankets, and the thick goose feather duvet. Hung them over the clothesline so that they flapped in the spring breeze like sails. But best of all, they cranked open the tall windows, so that the bigger world poured in through the screens and filled my room with yearning.

The Aunties weren't really aunts at all, but cleaning ladies, white-haired grannies hired to help Nana with the task of keeping house, now that I had been dropped into her care. She introduced them all to me as Auntie, and I called them such. Mildred, whom I never called Auntie, was my only authentic aunt. Nana's little sister, although the bigger sister in stature. Mildred, my aunt by bloodline, never turned down my bed, never washed my sheets, never cranked open my window – although she did take an unholy interest in my affairs.

As soon as I had grown big enough to pull myself up on the window ledge, I was no longer satisfied to sit upon the floor behind the curtain. Instead I sat for hours in the window. Then stared into the distance as far as I could see, and then much further than I could see, imagined the places beyond. I soon learned to crank open the window myself. Cranked the handle mightily. The wind that blew through the screen brought the sea into my room, I could smell it.

"You can't possibly smell it," they told me - a myriad of 'theys' had sprung into my life. "No matter what ocean you mean, the Arctic to the north, the Pacific to the west, the Atlantic to the east, the Caribbean to the South. They're all far, far away."

I didn't believe them. Sensed even as a child that distance was a matter of perception, personal inclination. A long journey for one is a short journey for another, hardly a journey at all. I *knew* the sea lay just beyond my window.

It didn't take me long to realize something else. If Pear could put the screen on and off, remove it in the autumn and return it in the spring, then so could I.

I located the latches against the window frame. Saw how they worked to hold the screen in place. Felt the power of those small contraptions, what they could do, how they could change destiny. Unlatched the screen, pulled it out. Wiggled the screen back in the window frame, until it fit just right, in perfect alignment, window and screen. Latched it in place.

But most of the time, I left the screen out.

Sat on the windowsill, way up high, above all else. I'd sit there, dangle my legs over the edge, tap-tap-tap my heels against the grey slate siding. Squirm closer to the edge, until only the smallest part of my body perched on the window ledge. Then I'd stretch my arms, and play the balancing game. And one day, in the midst of the game, I sniffed at the air and smelled the sea, felt the *tug*. That's when I ran away for the second time in my short life.

Pushed away from the windowsill and leapt into the wind.

Chapter 10

The moon is red and full and hazy outside the seminary window. The sky hangs thick with the fog, too, in the same colour, although the sun set hours ago. A dead tree stands in contrast to the fog, as if a cutout pasted to the front of it. Black trunk and thin branches glisten with rain changing to ice changing to rain. The temperature hovers near freezing, feeling indecisive, dropping just below, and then rising just above.

Windows line the only wall of the seminary library that is not lined by books. There are no latches on the windows, and no handles to crank. No way to open them up. The glass of the library window is thick and tightly sealed around the edges. To conserve energy, I suppose, or to stop disillusioned seminary students from jumping. Surely each one has a moment of doubt, his dark night of the soul. One should only hope.

Residue from my childhood, like other people seek nostalgic smells, bread baking in the oven, or catching a sniff of pine and thinking of Christmas. I notice windows, their mechanisms, how to open them. Check latches.

The library lights flicker, signaling the time for the seminary students to pack up and go home, and if not home, then just to go. I need a place to sleep, but I have a plan.

The hallway is empty. No one sees me slip into the women's washroom, shut the door softly behind me. This is a school of men. They forbid themselves the forbidden, wear their restraint in the way they hold their bodies, as if twice removed from them, a distant relative. There are no women here to find me hiding in the washroom, and no men who would push through a forbidden door to look to see if the room is empty. It's a perfect place to hide while the library empties.

When I think they've all left, I wait another minute, count to sixty slowly, and then leave the washroom. The library is pitch black, and I grope for a flashlight in my knapsack, turn it on. The flashlight casts an eerie light, and the feeling is familiar. Almost comforting, as much as I have ever felt comfort. I'm a little girl again, lying in the church, the altar candles casting their shadows into the emptiness.

Alone in the seminary, I read in the dark by the light of my flashlight, curled in my chair. I wish the chair could rock, but it does not, even though I rock my body, hear the distant sound of rockers against hardwood floor.

Soft against my memory, like a lullaby.

Chapter 11

"She *jumped*," Mildred whispered.

In actuality, Mildred screamed, not whispered, Nana said later, correcting my version of the story and counteracting Mildred's version. Screamed like a nincompoop banshee, Nana said, shaking her head and rotating her finger in a circular fashion to indicate her sister was crazy. Nana had a way with words, and with fingers.

To me, however, Mildred had whispered.

I thought I had realized my wish, and leapt the distance to the ocean, and lay on the sea bottom, miles of water above me, land voices muffled and faint and faraway.

Of course I jumped, I tried to say. The words rose from my mouth in air bubbles, popping to the surface like bubbles do. I watched them rush upwards and out of reach.

"She's gasping," someone said. "Give her room to breathe."

They say (and they had much to say about it,) that in "such situations" hearing is the last faculty to be lost and the first to return. Such situations, referring to children who jump out of third story windows and land with a thud on the ground.

If hearing returns first, then sight is second.

Faces loomed over me, but their edges seeped into each other. I squinted, tried to count them, and then, as the images grew sharper, to identify faces. There was Pear, face large and wavy, and less scowl-ish than usual.

"Mon Dieu, Mon Dieu," Pear repeated, voice like a foghorn. I wondered what it was he had to do. I felt clammy and cold, and I shivered.

"Make yourself useful, Mildred," Nana said, her face distorted in a circus-mirror kind of way. "The child is shaking. Give her your sweater, and stop blubbering."

Nana grabbed the sweater off Mildred.

"It's a miracle," Mildred cried, no longer a whisper. I thought maybe it was my life that was the miracle, but I was wrong. Life is not a miracle to Mildred.

"She *flew* to the ground, *fluttered* like a bird," Mildred said. "I saw her, with my own two eyes."

"Whose two eyes could you have seen it through, but your own?" Nana snapped.

If the pecking order of the senses is sound, and then sight, then touch surely follows. Pear scooped me up in his arms, and pain shot through my body. I had surfaced from the bottom of the ocean into the world from which I had leapt to escape, a place where sound was not muffled, and my own screams frightened me.

"Watch her leg," someone said, a lesser they. "The bone is sticking out."

And in there somewhere, between the pain and my own screams, layered with Pear's *Mon Dieu's*, and Nana's *shut-up's*, Mildred's voice floated in and out, as if her words were fluttering dimes.

"She flew," Mildred said. "A big invisible hand held her, and gently laid her down. It's a miracle."

So which is it? I want to ask Mildred, all these years later. Did I fly like a bird or did a Giant Hand intervene?

But Mildred is dead, so the asking would be difficult. And if she isn't dead, if I lie, then this is the truth. I will never ask these questions of Mildred. To do so, even by letter or phone or email, is to retrace my path, to return after I have left. And that, I will never do. Except perhaps for a raven-haired girl named Lily.

Chapter 12

I've lived in the library for a week now, long enough for the regulars to nod their head in my direction. And once, when I sneezed, I received a "God Bless". I shouldn't be surprised. This is a seminary, after all, although the blessing sounded suspiciously unholy coming from the mouth of a kid who might just as easily have said 'yo ho fuck bitch.' He must be preparing for a youth ministry, I thought, dreadlocks and baggy drawstring pants down around his hips and air-pumped, big-soled running shoes, or maybe he has come here to get out of the cold. We've latched on to the same scam, two barnacles to the same hull.

I haven't left the seminary since the first night. There is no reason. The library meets my immediate needs, both for shelter and nourishment. I don't talk in metaphor, waxing poetically about spiritual nourishment. The library provides *physical* nourishment, actual sustenance. Food appears, like manna dropped from heaven. Carefully cut into one-meal portions and neatly wrapped.

The manifestations come in odd places, as if they've been misplaced or accidentally toppled from the ideal lunchbox. It starts simply enough.

First there is the apple on the trolley where the books are left for re-stacking. It sits there innocently, as if just fallen from the tree, but as anyone who has read Genesis knows, an apple is not innocent. I grabbed the apple quickly, stuffed it into my bag, gloated at my fortune.

Next came a bran muffin with a walnut on top. It miraculously appeared nestled in a row of concordances. You might think I would have been suspicious, finding a muffin next to the concordances. But I was hungry.

The manifestations grow more complex. Carrot and celery sticks hand-cut and peeled, with a little tub of spinach dip, left with a serviette on the armrests of my chair. Chocolate granola bars leaning against my knapsack. An alfalfa sprouts and Swiss cheese sandwich, made from whole wheat bread and spread thinly with mustard, on a nearby study table. A small bottle of freshly squeezed orange juice next to my book on Church Fathers, and another time, apple juice. All carefully wrapped and nutritiously balanced, as if planned around a list of the recommended daily nutrients for healthy living.

At first I thought the street-preacher-in-training must be using me as target practice for his good works. Ministering to the street kid who squatters in the seminary. It takes me three full days to realize it is the Saint of the Uneaten Bagel.

I hadn't suspected him. He stays close, too obvious to be the obvious, the wise fool. The Saint has a name. Thomas.

I search it out on the inside of his textbooks. Both his name and his handwriting are formal. He's never just Tom. He never prints, always writes. The black ink of his new dime store ballpoint flows across the page, letters never varying in height or slant, all listing uniformly starboard. The bottom margin of his name is absolutely straight and within the lines, although there are no lines. He just writes as if there are. I suspect at the time he lives that way, too.

Thomas leaves food for me as if I'm a bird or a wild animal. He thinks he tames me. That soon I'll eat from his hand. Peck at the seed. Nuzzle the apple slices from his flat palm, like a deer that has come out of the woods in winter because it is starving.

But Thomas is wrong. Stupidly wrong.

No one tames me.

By the sixth day, I know that Thomas knows that I know. We prolong the charade. This night, the eighth night, I head towards the women's washroom, as usual. The lights have flashed. It's time for lockdown.

Thomas blocks the door. A brave act, and also a stupid one. I have a knife.

"You can't stay here forever," he says.

Of course not, I don't stay anywhere forever.

"I'm Thomas," he explains. "If you need a place to crash, you can stay with me."

"Thomas, like the Aquinas," I answer.

And I go with him.

Chapter 13

I'm tired of the broken leg, tired of the cast. Tired of how it keeps me stationary, how it makes me dependent upon the Aunties. How they dress me, move me, decide when it's time for me to eat. And every morning, cart me to where they decide I should sit. Deposit me in the garden to watch the birds, and I can do nothing, but watch the birds. I hate it. I want to be a secret again. To sit in my windowsill, to hang from an open window if I wish, to fall from it if that is what happens. To do what I want, when I want.

Nana assigns Pear the job of keeping me occupied. By that, she means sitting in the garden and watching the birds. Pointing out the varieties, teaching me to tell the difference between the male of a species and the female, the difference in the plumage of the Eastern Phoebe and an Eastern Wood-Peewee. I have no patience. Birds fly. That I can admire. They have the ability to escape. The rest is detail.

The wheelbarrow is Pear's idea. Even now, I love Pear for it. It is good to love him, when I have felt so much hate. As if it were his fault, the lies and the truths, worn inside out like a shirt.

He scoops me off the thick soft lazy lawn chair, his

eyes wicked with the pleasure of disobeying Nana, and I feel his heart race against my skin. He places me carefully in the wheelbarrow, doesn't bother to clean out the dirt and leaves and twigs in the bottom. I like the dirt and leaves and twigs against my too-clean clothes, scuffing the brilliant white of the cast. First Pear walks, and then trots, and then runs. I spur him on with my shrieks. *More, more, faster, faster,* I tell him, delirious with the motion.

The leg that is broken, my left leg, is propped up over the edge of the wheelbarrow, juts out like a butting log. I'm harnessed in a cast from hip to big toe. I hear Pear's thick panting. He pushes me around the circular driveway, as best as he can, although I wish for more speed, always more speed.

The wheelbarrow bounces over the gravel, sending up a thin spray of dust, stone flying like shrapnel. Every once in a while, Pear spits out the word Nana forbids him to say, "Merde." His flat shoes go pat-pat-pat against the driveway, and I can tell from the rhythm of the sound when he slows his pace. "Faster, faster," I shout, as if Pear is a racehorse.

It doesn't occur to me that Pear might collapse. He is a white-haired man with thickening joints and a belly that hangs over his belt. He doesn't exercise, except in fits and starts, odd handyman jobs around the manor, changing the screen windows, or hauling second-hand goods into the station wagon and out again. Huffing and puffing, face red with exertion, he never stops until the job is done, or the item is where he wants it to be, lugged into the garage, or basement, or in a corner of the yard. Then he sits down, gulping breaths, eyes bulging, sweat rolling down his face.

"Mee-kel-la, surely you rest now," Pear finally says.

"No," I yell.

To appease me, to satisfy my cravings, Pear spins in circles. Slow at first, to catch his breath, to find his balance, to adjust to dizziness, and then gaining speed, *faster, faster,* until all is a blur.

Suddenly the motion stops.

Nana stands above me, hands on her hips.

Her eyes flare, and pink flashes across her cheeks.

"You could have a heart attack," she tells Pear. "You old coot, and look at Michaela, she is flushed with excitement, she will get a fever, she is so frail as it is."

Pear is too breathless to protest, so he doesn't say anything. I protest for him.

"His heart wouldn't attack."

Pear manages to smile. He hits his chest with his fist, and says, "Le coeur, stay brave of heart, little one."

Nana picks me up. She holds me like an infant. Cuddles me in her arms and close to her breast. It bothers me that I am so small, so weightless, that Nana can carry me this way, even with the cast, so I tense my body. Try to make myself heavy.

"You are a twig," she says. And then, "I will find something harmless to keep you busy, Michaela, where even you cannot hurt yourself, cannot get into trouble, my little wild cat."

My little wild cat.

I like that, and for once, let my body ease in her arms.

Chapter 14

The Saint of the Uneaten Bagel lives in a boarding house.

The fact surprises me. I thought he'd live in the seminary residence. Eat communal dinner in silence with a long row of men set on the same path of redemption and celibacy. Sleep in a single bed beside another single bed in a dormitory where the men rise before dawn to pray in the chapel.

An empty beer bottle sits in the hallway, and unclaimed flyers lay strewn across the floor. My clothes are wet; the rain has soaked through to my skin. My knapsack feels heavy, and I'm tired and cold. I shake off discomfort and scold myself to stay alert. Survival depends upon it, and if not my survival, then at least a place to stay the night, and some food in my stomach, and a wallet or drawer to ransack.

We trudge the steps to the third floor. The hallway is dark, and a bulb needs to be replaced somewhere. Thomas leads the way. He opens a door. Fumbles his palm along the wall. Light floods the room. It is just that, a single room. Nothing more, not even a washroom. There must be a shared bath at the end of the hallway. The Saint lives communal, after all.

An open box of apple-oat granola bars sits on the counter, and a bag of multi-grain bagels, and an overripe banana, and sesame seed crackers. I realize with a start that these are the foods that Thomas has fed to me at the library.

I'm not sure why that realization startles me. I knew it was Thomas who had left the food, scattered across my days like breadcrumbs for the birds, so the reaction wasn't a matter of revelation, a whodunit solved. Rather, I think it was the sum total. One item piled against another, against another, against another. Like fact, upon fact, upon fact, or even lies. Pile them up together, look at them all at once, and they say something much different than when viewed separately, each in its own time and place.

I suppose the pile on Thomas's counter underscored his effort, the length to which he had gone. There is a hot plate on the counter, and a small bar fridge next to a card table. Salt and pepper shakers sit side by side in front of a plastic place mat. An ivy plant, remarkably green, trails off the side of a dresser.

A small crucifix hangs on the wall, and on the desk, among the papers and books, a black and white photo of a young boy, freckles and front teeth gone, sitting on a stoop with an old man. They have that look that stares out of old pictures. It's a bravely vulnerable look, as if they know something I don't, and that something sits there, right behind the smile. Or maybe I have it wrong. It is the reverse. Maybe it is that I know something that they do not, and that is why they look that way, so vulnerably brave.

The photo of the old man and the boy, the crucifix, even the salt and pepper shakers. These are Thomas's attempt at creating home. I understand, in some strange way, and feel an unlikely kinship with him.

Thomas's room is tidy, and I am startled for the second time. It strikes me that he straightened it in anticipation of my arrival. Prepared for me to come, even before I had agreed. I think about that. Imagine it. Thomas, methodically sweeping crumbs into a pile in the center of the floor, sweeping the pile into a dustbin, sweeping the tail of dust that lingers across the floor, sweeping the cobwebs that collect in the corners. Wiping the counter clean, the sink. Washing his socks, matching them, rolling them together, washing his underwear, putting it away so that the plastic laundry basket sits empty in the corner, and the room is tidy.

I lay my knapsack down. Water slides off and to the floor. My shoes leave wet spots.

"Forgive me," Thomas says (how like a seminary student to seek forgiveness). "Come in, get dried off. It's not much, but you're welcome to stay here until you find another place."

He throws me a towel, and then pulls out a flannel shirt and sweatpants from a drawer. "You can wear these," he says, tossing the clothes on his bed.

The bed is actually a fold-up cot. Room for one.

Thomas rubs his head with a towel so that his hair stands up. It looks good on him, spiked - less saintly. I want to laugh aloud at the transformation, but stop myself. Thomas isn't ready for laughter. There is order to seduction.

I pull my hood down off my head, wipe my face with the towel, and then rub my own hair. It, too, is unruly, but naturally so. I see myself in the mirror of Thomas's dresser. Yellow tufts clump together like stubs of drought grass. He lays the towel over the back of the folding card chair to dry.

"Hungry?" he asks.

"Have you ever known me not to be?" I answer.

Thomas smiles at the absurdity of his question. There is no other room in which to change. I move slowly, pull the sweatshirt over my head, stand there for a moment, so that Thomas has time to become aware of shape. I am wearing an undershirt, but it is tight. The lines are clear. The geography of body. I see my reflection in the mirror, and I know he can see it, too. My skin is pale, and I look smaller without the sweatshirt to hide me. Younger, too. There is a small blue wave tattooed across my shoulder, and I wonder if Thomas has noticed.

I take off the undershirt.

This is the moment around which all else revolves. I watch Thomas carefully. If he is startled at whom he has brought home, one with tits rather than a cock and balls, he doesn't show it. I wait for him to react, throw me out of his room, but he doesn't. I reach for the flannel shirt he has given me to wear, pull my arms into the sleeves, do up the buttons. The shirt is large and my shape is lost again. I roll up the cuffs so that my fingers show. Pull off my rain-drenched pants. The hem of the flannel shirt stretches past my knees. My legs look scrawny, not the legs of a temptress.

Thomas must have thought the same.

He turns away from me, squats down, opens the fridge, examines the contents, busies himself with cheese and butter and lettuce and bread.

Chapter 15

Nana carries a cardboard box. She has more difficulty carrying the box than she had carrying me. She's bent over with the weight, steps with tiny shuffles, and I think she'll send the contents spilling across the floor. She half-drops, half-places the box on the Persian rug. Expels it, almost, and then stops to catch her breath. She recovers quickly, has much less breath to catch than Pear.

It doesn't take long before Nana is moving again. She takes the vase of fresh lilacs from the coffee table, and puts the vase on the mantle next to the photo of the pale man with the fair hair. Then Nana drags the box towards me. I stretch to peer inside, twist my body as far as I can, wrapped up in a plaster cast and lying on the couch. She's slow, and I'm impatient with her. Finally she drags the box until I can see in it.

I am disappointed.

Nana lacks imagination, I tell myself. That's why she's brought me such useless things. What could I expect from her? Nana is old, and ugly, and land-bound. She's a fusser over gardens, and fruit trees, and lilac bushes, and cedar trees. A fusser over pots, and planters, and flower boxes, containers that sprout leaves and blossoms from every sunny spot of the house. She sends plant life tumbling from old boots and teapots and barrels and bowls, sprouting from every windowsill. She talks to her plants, sings them love songs. Never love songs for my dead mother and me. Just for her plants. She doesn't seem to know; they don't run away, because they can't. They're bound to the spot.

Like Nana's plants, I too am bound to this spot, but by this cast. It's all that keeps me here, on this couch and in this house. It's just a matter of time before I run away again. I know this, even as a child.

Bound words! This is what she has brought me. Nana spreads *books* across the coffee table. The books are musty and the covers have stains on them. The pages are faded yellow and trimmed around the edges in brown, as if they've been dipped in a vat of cooking grease. These books must be as old as Nana.

"There," Nana says, with satisfaction, even smugness, as if all problems have been solved, and she has solved them. And then she leaves the room.

I pick up a book. Open it. The symbols mean nothing to me, I can't read. I put the book down, pick up another.

This one is brightly colored, each page a patchwork puzzle of pink and green and yellow and blue. It's the blue that fascinates me. I yell for Nana.

Shove the book at her.

"What's this?" I demand.

"An atlas, Michaela."

"At last," I echo, as if I've finally found what I've been searching.

Nana sits next to me. Turns the book the other way. Takes my finger. Points to the four tips of the compass. "North, South, East, West," she says, making the sign of the cross with my finger on the page, as if we are in church, and I understand well enough that this book is holy.

"North is always up," Nana tells me, touching the top of the page with my fingertip. "Look for North and the rest will follow. See? N, S, E, W. Repeat after me," and I repeat.

And so I learn to situate myself to the compass, to

the North, like a true traveller. Learn to say the letters of the alphabet, not ABC, in alphabetical order, but NSEW, the four cardinal directions.

Nana continues her lessons. She flattens my small hand, brushes my palm against the page in a circular motion. "This is a map," she says.

"What good is a map?" I ask.

"They are routes to other places," she tells me.

My heart quickens. I know now what Pear means, *be brave of heart.* "And why is the map blue?"

"That is the ocean," Nana says.

"How do I get to the ocean from here?"

Nana squints, peers closely at the map as if she is searching. "Ah," she says, relaxing her face. "Here we are," and she touches a dot in the middle of the page. I'm in awe of the map, in awe of this dot, that a dot on a map can hold a whole house, hold geography, hold *me.*

It's a game we play each day until my leg mends.

Nana sets me on the sofa, and I screech "At last! At last!" and she gives me the book of maps.

I open it randomly to a page, maybe Africa, or Europe, or the Middle East, or South America. I close my eyes, and stab my finger down hard and say, "How do I get to the ocean from *here*?"

And Nana would trace the route, naming the countries, and towns, and rivers, and lakes along the way, naming the equator, or the Tropic of Capricorn, or the dateline, or whatever line ran through it. Naming the particular ocean.

This is how I learn to read, the words that teach me the ways of language and the secrets of books. Not child's words, not cat and dog and mouse and teddy bear and mommy and daddy, but the words of the traveller.

It's ironic that I'm taught by an old woman who is land-bound. Rooted to her particular spot, her particular rock, her particular garden. But to Nana, it is just a game.

To me, it is the world.

Chapter 16

Thomas fusses, trying to be quiet. He doesn't want to disturb me. He sets the grocery bag on the counter as if it might make a noise, talk too loud or burp. His actions are either sweet or annoying. I haven't decided yet.

"Don't you have seminary classes?" I ask.

My question startles Thomas. His body jumps. Doesn't he know I might have something to say? Maybe he hasn't thought that far ahead yet. Hasn't thought of me beyond a cause, his charitable act. Rescue the boy who turns out to be a girl. Like putting the bowl of milk out for the cat, and the cat sticks around, refuses to leave, and all you thought you were doing was putting a bowl of milk out for the cat.

I push myself up, swing my legs around so I sit cross-legged on the bed.

"Classes are done for the day," Thomas says, composure regained. "It's mid-afternoon."

Thomas slept on the couch last night. His blankets are neatly folded and stacked at one end. Mine fall around me, tumble messily to the floor.

The springs in the couch are broken, and the cushions sink in a mold of Thomas's body. The couch is short, his arms and legs must have hung over the sides. I don't know, fell asleep quickly, hadn't realized I was so tired, how good it would feel to stretch out on a bed, even a cot.

Thomas treads softly in his socks. They're matching socks, no less. And no holes. Socks say a lot about a person. Thomas's socks tell me he is domesticated, lives life in one spot. He's organized, predictable. Most tellingly, he's not a traveller. A traveller doesn't care if her socks are matched. Laundromats are her hunting grounds, where abandoned socks seldom come in matching pairs.

"What can I get you?" Thomas asks. "Cereal, eggs, toast, waffles, blueberry muffin, fruit, coffee, orange juice, tea?"

"Sure," I say. Let him feed me.

Thomas pauses. I can see his mind work. He thinks to ask which I want, which item on his breakfast menu, and then thinks again. Simply fiddles. Cracks eggs into a pan, stirs. Fiddles some more. Chops mushrooms, cheese, peppers.

"What's your name?" Thomas asks.

My name must be the price for breakfast.

"Mary," I lie.

"Ah," Thomas smiles. "Like the sister of Martha."

"Wrong Mary."

Thomas pours me a glass of orange juice. He's giving me my daily-recommended dosage of Vitamin C. He wouldn't want me to get scurvy. I'm sure Thomas thinks of those things. It goes back to his socks.

"Ah, like the Virgin Mary, then," Thomas quips.

I smile. He has a sense of humor. The saintly façade cracks.

Thomas slips an omelet from the frying pan onto a plate centered on the plastic flower placemat.

"Eat," he says.

My stomach rumbles. I move to the card table, do what he tells me to do.

Eat. Finish it all. Wipe my plate clean with a piece of bread, eat the piece of bread. Then I speak.

"No, not Mary, like the Virgin Mary. And anyway, what makes you so sure she was a virgin?" I ask.

My question sits there. Thomas picks up my dishes. Puts them in the sink. Fills it with water. Squirts in soap, swishes the dishwater with his hand to make it bubble. I pursue the virgin issue. Won't let him off the hook so easily.

"Mary had children - plural," I bait. "Do you think they were all immaculately conceived?"

Thomas washes my plate. Traces the dishcloth around the outer rim. Sets the plate upright in the dishpan to dry. Fishes in the dirty dishwater. Snags a coffee cup. Sticks the dishcloth deep into it, swishes his hand around, removes himself from the cup, puts it upside down to dry beside the plate. Fishes again. He is ignoring me.

"Let's see," I continue, counting on my fingers. "James, and Joseph, and Simon, and Judas, that's four. And then all the sisters, if we take as gospel truth the words of Matthew and Mark. That's a womb full of children for a virgin."

The bait works. Thomas can't resist. After all, he's a seminary student. He wipes his hands on the dishcloth, hangs the dishcloth over the stove handle to dry. I see his mind working, argument running through the circuitry of his brain, thoughts organizing themselves into a reasoned response. I speak just before his words get a chance to leave his voice box. "Some say the Koine, the ancient Greek, means kinsmen. Those who believe in the Virgin Birth would claim the translation is cousin, and not brother and sister."

I have beaten him to his arguments. I gloat. "But then, scholars debate everything, don't they? Some men find red lipstick a turn-on, others prefer ideas."

Thomas smiles. The smile puts me off-guard. "How do you know so much?" he asks.

"I'm homeless, not stupid," I retort.

Thomas's smile dissolves. "I wasn't implying you are stup—"

"Sure you were."

Red sweeps his cheeks, his neck.

Time to let up on Thomas.

"How do I know so much? I've been living in a seminary library for a week. Not much else to do besides read and steal bagels."

Thomas smiles again, that lop-sided half-smile. It broadsides me, like a rogue wave. "Which Mary are you, then, if not the Virgin or Martha's sister?"

"Mary Magdalene," I tell Thomas.

He laughs aloud. Can't help himself, can't imagine me in the role of wanton woman. I laugh, too. It's true, I don't look the part, but things are not always as you think.

I consider him fairly warned.

Chapter 17

Each time I asked for my mother as a child, my grandfather brought me a silver picture frame from the mantelpiece with the photograph of the washed-out pale man. Put it to my face, and said "pear, pear, pear."

At first, I was perplexed. I thought he didn't understand me, and I'd say the word again. Try the many variations to make my wishes known. Mama. Mother. Mom. Ma. Even mére, when I grew a little older. And still he wouldn't tell me about her. Nana, neither. Nor the Aunties, nor even Mildred, who usually had too much to say. They cast their glances to the ground, grew terribly busy with something else, gave me diversions, a nickel or a kiss. I spurned their kisses, but took their nickels. Saved them in a big empty mustard jar hidden in the closet of my room.

At first, I longed for my mother in the flesh and blood. Then, I simply longed to have them say her name. To hear them speak of her aloud to me. But they refused to say the words, so I said her name aloud to myself. Sometimes I would climb into the rocking chair and sing her name as if it were a lullaby. Sometimes I would whisper it, pull myself on the windowsill and give her name to the wind. Sometimes I would cry her name, wipe my eyes on the corner of the curtain. Sometimes I would scream her name, throw myself to the ground, kick and bite and pound my rage.

I pestered my grandfather the most of all. If I stayed the course, refused to deviate, kept after him, I thought he would submit to my demands, tell me about my mother. It had worked for the storm windows. But instead, he grew larger and angrier, like an ocean storm. Waved the photo in my face, roared about his precious pears. My fury grew as well, and I matched him storm by storm. I swelled with rage that he refused to bring me my mother, in real life or in memory.

I stomped into the kitchen, reached for the fruit bowl on the table. Made myself grow the bit I lacked, stretched some more, and then my fingers caught the rim. I pulled the bowl towards me, yanked it angrily so that it fell. Fruit spilled over my head like rain, and the bowl crashed against the floor, scattering bits and pieces across the room.

I crawled under the table, shards digging into my knees, but I didn't feel anything, so great my anger. Crawled straight to the fruit that had slid to rest against the foot of the table, the table leg like the paw of a great animal. Found another piece in the corner under the china cabinet. Clutched a piece of fruit in each hand. Stormed back to the living room. Gave my grandfather what he had been asking for, took aim and fired. First one pear, and then the other.

The smacks to the forehead, rat-a-tat-tat, didn't knock any sense into my grandfather. Still he insisted upon pears. Just pears, as if they were the only fruit in the world. I thought him crazy.

For every pear he spoke, I asked about my mother. And finally, I asked as much to drive him more insane, as to hear him speak her name. Such was the madness of his ranting, directed solely at me. As if *I* were the one who refused to understand, refused to remember.

"Leave her alone," Nana said to him early one morning, taking me by the hand and leading me away. They exchanged angry words in a language I didn't understand.

"Pierre, Pierre, you are a stubborn old fool, and Michaela

is but a child."

Pierre. Pierre. Pear. Pear.

It struck me full force.

He was Pear-Pear, as certainly as I was Michaela.

I pulled away from Nana, ran to him.

"Pear-pear," I cried, and his face lit with exquisite joy at my understanding.

He swept me into his arms, and hugged me close, and then he kissed me, a smack that resounded throughout the room like a booming cannon.

I had never seen him so happy, and would never see him that way again. Happiness, like so much else, is a traveller, doesn't put down root and stay in a single place.

The length of our happiness, Pear-pear's and mine, was one full day. And then our happiness dwindled, not taking leave all at once, but bit by bit, like water draining from a pond.

A drop or two left every time I tugged him by the trousers and called him by his name. Every time I shouted Pear-pear from my window, and waved at him with giant brushstrokes of my arm. Every time I called for him to come to me, a hundred times that day at least. I cried Pear-pear this, Pear-pear that.

Pear-pear, will you tie my shoelaces, double knot them so they won't come undone? Pear-pear, play catch with me? Pick flowers in the garden? Dig worms from the compost heap? Pear-pear, you can answer me in your funny language, it doesn't matter, because we are happy.

That evening, he summoned me.

Mee-kel-la, Mee-kel-la, he called in his peculiar way, as if the syllables of my name didn't fit together right, didn't quite belong.

I followed the sound of his voice and found him in the living room. Pear-pear stood by the fireplace, staring at the photograph on the mantelpiece. His face was white, and he looked tired and sad. I understood the sadness, if not the fatigue.

Pear-pear sighed when he saw me, a heavy sigh that

settled into the room. He reached for the same picture frame as always, and sat down with it in his armchair. He motioned with a wave of his fingers for me to come to him, and I did.

Pear-pear patted his knee, and I climbed up on top of it. He touched the image of the pale bland man in the photo. Prolonged the touch as if to emphasize it. Then he touched his own chest. Repeated the action. Photo to chest. Photo to chest.

"Père," he said, each time he tapped himself. He spoke gravely, softly. No more storms.

And then Pear-pear sat still, waiting for something to happen.

But nothing did, so he continued his game.

He touched my chest, slightly to the left, as if to point out my heart. Then he touched the photo, touched the face of the moon-colored man peering out of it. He spoke solemnly, said "père" with every touch of the glass. He repeated the action, repeated the word, three times.

I threw the frame to the floor, and ran from the room. Ran into the yard as far as I could run and climbed the biggest tree. Climbed sturdy limb to sturdy limb, until the branches grew thin, and bent with my slight weight.

And still I climbed, to the very top, where I swayed with the tip of the tree, and wailed with the wind into the night.

Never again did I ask about my mother. Not of my grandfather, or the others in the family. Never again did he talk to me about pears, of any kind or spelling. Never again did he bring me the framed photo of the pale blonde-haired man. He left it where it sat on the mantelpiece, a crack across the glass from the fall.

I continued to call him Pear-pear, refused to call him anything else. And when I grew older, seven or eight, I simply called him Pear.

Chapter 18

Imagine it is 1240.

Thomas Aquinas, the future Saint, now just a boy, hunches at his desk. He keeps himself like that, all day long, and all night long, cooped up in a small room at the top corner of the family's ancestral home. Why he insists upon that room when there were others much bigger, and more comfortably furnished, and with more pleasing views of the estate, his mother can't fathom.

She thinks she knows her son. What is there to know? The mind of her youngest son pierces to the center of things like the blade of a newly whetted knife, and he has a fine head for details. If he'd only apply it to numbers and the family finances, instead of the church and dead philosophers, she thinks, and this silly idea about entering a monastery. He needs to learn there are other things in life besides books and the church. Not *learn*, she corrects herself. He's done enough *learning* in his short life for twenty men of full age. *Experience.* He needs to *experience* there are other things in life besides books and the church.

"Arrange a woman for Thomas," she tells her oldest son, Cochrane.

Six hours later Cochrane is back, straw in his hair.

"Simone," he says. "She'll visit Thomas tonight in his room as he studies."

*****

That evening, while working by candlelight, scrunched over his manuscripts, Thomas Aquinas feels a breath, soft and seductive against his neck, and thinks it is the Holy Spirit.

He closes his eyes, distracted by the perfume that fills the room. He thinks the aroma *is* God, in ghost form, the smell of a thousand roses. He has heard about miracles where rose petals, as bright as blood, fall from the sky like drops of rain. He sighs with the sweet delight of God as touch, God as perfume. "Thy will be done," Thomas Aquinas murmurs.

Upon the words of consent, Thomas Aquinas feels the touch of a hand. He spins around, sees Simone dancing for him, like Salome for Herod. Anger roars through his body. He sends his chair tumbling across the room. Grabs the iron from the fire, circles it above his head like a sword, his eyes burning.

Simone flees.

Like Lot's wife, she looks back. But unlike Lot's wife, she lives to tell the tale. Tells the others, the townsfolk and the household servants, what she saw. Young Thomas, wild and angry, a John-the-Baptist in the desert, searing the sign of the cross into the wood of his bedroom door.

*****

Thomas Aquinas fell to his knees and wept. Not because Simone had come to his room, but because he had mistaken her for the Holy Ghost. Had thought the scent and breath and whisper of a woman had been the scent and breath and whisper of God. And when he had finished weeping, Thomas packed his most prized books and manuscripts in a small sack. Ran off to the monastery. Found refuge, found home, in ideas.

Chapter 19

"Mary!"

I've slipped easily into the name. Thomas doesn't know that I am any other, and I never tell him. If he looks for me, even now, he looks for Mary.

In my dreams, I calculate velocity, the effect of the wind on my body, how I must compensate, trust my physical reactions. I flap from the windowsill of Thomas's room. I feel no fear or hesitation, only the surge of adrenaline. It is my way.

"Mary!"

The sound pulls me from the windowsill and back into bed. I sit up, push the sleep from my eyes. It's late morning, and the winter sun glares through the glass. Smaller panes form the larger window and I think the building must have once been a factory. Snow collects in the corner of each window, as if one pane is a photocopy of the other, and I wonder which is the original, in that way you wonder things at the edge of sleep that make no sense when you're awake.

I've lived with Thomas for two months now, long enough for autumn to turn into winter. I don't have boots or coat or mitts and hat, and don't need them. I seldom leave the room, and when I do, I wear Thomas's. His clothes have become my clothes, his things my things.

Even his bed is mine, although we don't share it. Thomas and I haven't yet touched. I don't see desire for touch in his body, although I hear it in his words, his voice. Desire not for the touch of my fingers upon his skin, but for the touch of my fingers upon his mind.

"Look what I have brought you, Mary," he says.

Thomas speaks with such exuberance. He is so easily exuberant, and his mood is infectious.

The snow from his boots gathers on the floor in small puddles, mid-transformation, half-snow, half-water. It is so unlike him not to carefully remove his boots, put them on the boot rack, take off his coat and hang it from the hook on the back of the door, place his mitts on the register to dry.

Thomas holds out a book to me. It's a slim volume, a new book. He has bought it, something he can't afford to do.

"For you," he says.

He has taken to the habit of feeding me books in the same manner he once fed me morsels of food. He leaves the books for me to find when he is at seminary. He rations them in palatable portions, one or two at a time, in well-balanced and digestible servings.

Thomas chooses reputable books, in Pygmalion fashion, for my education. No dubious research, no ill-conceived arguments, no junk food of scholarship. Never too much of one food, however healthy, never all cherries or oranges or bananas, but a sampling of each on my plate. Never too much of one author or viewpoint - not only Thomas Aquinas, but also Thomas the Doubter.

The books simply appear, as if it's natural for the night table to sprout a copy of *Gospel Parallels*. Or the placemat to hold excerpts of the *Theological Summa*. Or to find *The Divine Milieu* propped against my coffee mug. Or *The Inferno* resting on my pillow.

It's this action, this choosing and leaving of books, which endears Thomas to me. That, and his kindness. Kindness can be deadly. I wonder if I'm the victim of deception, if the seductress is not the seduced. I think Thomas incapable, but perhaps that's only delusion.

The books connect the two of us where there's little other connection. I understand books. They're a portal to places. A way to run away. Books are the mode of escape - the ship, the plane, the train - and the destination, too.

Thomas leaves fluorescent Post-it notes flapping from the margins like tiny flags. The bright colors are an extravagance for Thomas, he's living on the edge. They beckon me, but that is all. There is no commentary on them, and I must guess to what particular idea Thomas directs me. He refuses to write on the pages of a book even with pencil. He says it's an affront to the book, as if written words are alive and can be hurt.

Me, I write in the margins. Highlight passages in yellow, pink, green. Comment in ink. Intrude, cross boundaries. Make a book my own. Travel it without holding back.

Thomas does not intrude, does not cross boundaries. He holds back. He's a dam. But then, dams have been known to break.

"Look what I've brought you," Thomas is saying, his voice alight. "Fourth century, apocryphal, part of the Nag Hammadi collection, the scroll discovered in a cave in Egypt in 1945, stuffed in an earthenware jar."

I take the book from him.

Hold it in my hands, feel it, open it up, begin my travelling. It's a physical action, the process of reading a book. I'm not one to stay motionless.

I read the title. *The Gospel of Thomas.*

Chapter 20

Nana sighs, looks at me as if the world is flat. By now, we'd surely reached the end. Sailed off the edge. "Not again," she says wearily when we reach the last page, and I flip to the first again. "Pick another book, Michaela," she says. "Not the atlas again. I am sick of maps."

So I pick.

Another book not much different by the cover, but looks can lie and covers can be deceiving. The choice pleases Nana. I, too, am pleased, because it means she'll read some more, grant me longer escape from my confinement.

I follow the written words on the page as she says them aloud. Pretend I do, if nothing more. I recognize random words in the print that Nana reads. Come to understand that the words travel from left to right, and start over again, trek their way down the page, top to bottom. Then I realize it's not the words that travel, but the story itself. A single word is fixed to its spot. The story, now, the story soars, sails the width and height and depth of a book. Travels far beyond. It's an epiphany, and I'm enthralled by the ease in which the story escapes the pages, listen to Nana as if she's caught by magic. I know these travels of which she speaks do not come from her mind, her imagination. She's incapable of such journeys. She is rooted like her plants.

If it might be said that the *"At Last!"* was my first lover, then it must also be said that it was not my last. Another book leaves its image upon me like a fingerprint in wax. Between the maps, I come back to this other book, until it is no longer just a story, but more real than real. And then, it *is* my real.

As Nana reads, I hear the long road echoed in the stories. Stories filled with bright color, and exaggeration. The tales capture my imagination, but it's the illustration in the midst of the book that sets my heart dancing. Sets it to flamenco, beating in sharp staccato, heels rapping against the hard floor.

Nana turns the page, and there it is, unexpectedly. Not the thick black typesetting that I had come to expect, where I search for words that I recognize, work to break the code, the ticket of passage that will allow me to travel the stories on my own.

This page gleams white. Shines as if it's been polished, not pale and yellow like the others. A woman dances on it, one arm above her head, and one arm by her waist. There is freedom here, a perfect insolence, and that is her attraction. Scorn in her eyes, and haughtiness in her carriage.

I envy her, in the way a child envies her mother. I gaze at her in awe, and she smiles at me, winks. We're comrades in this dance. Her skirts swirl about my face like bright sails, and I hear the rockers against the wood. I sit on the floor and choose colour like sacrament, a crimson crayon as red as blood. Truth and memory mix like blood brothers, fingers sliced and open wounds pressed together.

Soon, I don't need Nana, tell the stories to myself, in my best reading voice, with all the drama and flair that the gypsy woman deserves. The adventures of her journey, her valour, her dancing, and when I know I have run out of words, have reached the bottom of the page, having watched Nana do the same in the same amount of time, I turn the page, and tell myself another story…

Chapter 21

I take Thomas's coat and boots, and go into the world. He doesn't notice, lost in his studies. He writes on a lined yellow notepad, each word perfectly formed in thought and script.

Thomas won't put a word to ink until he has first put the word to mind. Chosen it deliberately, committed himself to it. He is big on commitment. Thomas believes in it. Not as an anchor around the neck, like it is to me, but as something light, something that floats. I haven't figured it out, haven't yet figured Thomas out, but when I do, it will be time to leave.

The boots are large, and I curl my toes to keep from stepping out of them. The coat fits just fine. I'm thin, but so is Thomas. The snow falls in thick petals around me, as if the wind carries white blossoms from another place. I feel a yearning for these other places, the dots on the map.

I buy candles, fat ones that stand on their own without holders. Fat candles of various heights and colours and aromas, and then small white tea lights in silver containers. And I buy wine, red wine.

How can Thomas refuse red wine and candles? Surely it's against his religion to refuse, some seminary oath he has taken and signed with his blood.

When I return, Thomas is reading aloud what he has written. He is animated when he is engaged in thinking, and his body responds to the nuances of thought.

Thomas uses his hands to make a point, then drops his hands into his lap, conceding the point. He chuckles softly. He speaks as if he addresses someone, an audience of one, but there is no other.

I set the candles around the room, and then strike a match. Light a candle, and light another candle, until the match burns my fingers. Drop the charred match into the sink, and it sizzles.

Thomas puts down his yellow pad of paper. Gives me his full attention, as if I am one of his ideas. Watches me. I like the watching. I light another match. Feel the striking beneath my fingertips. It is a feeling you wouldn't notice unless you pay attention to it, commit to the noticing. Velvet, the smooth striking of the match.

The flame leaps and I light another candle. Use that candle to light the rest. Travel through the room, candle in hand, and candle to candle, aware of body, aware of Thomas's watching.

Twist the cork from the bottle. Pour wine. Hand a glass to Thomas. Turn off the lamp. Sit on the floor at his feet, and wait.

It's a comfortable silence, a comfortable waiting. Stars mark the night sky outside the window, and stars, like candles, mark the darkened room, too. I slip into the comfort. Sip wine. Lean against Thomas.

Thomas touches his hand to my hair. Slides his hand to the base of my neck. His touch is brief like a passing thought. He moves to the floor, sits beside me. Looks into my face. Talks softly, but with intent. Dances for me. Dances ideas. What he knows, and what he believes. Tells me about books he has read, thoughts he has had, lectures he has attended at the seminary. Talks to me about philosophers, thinkers, teachers, travellers of the mind. It's seductive, our talk.

Thomas is animated and alive. He asks about what I've read, and what I think about the passages he has marked with his bright Post-it flags. It's foreplay, cerebral lovemaking. He listens to my words. Explores me, responds to what he learns, no less than if we touched. More than if we touched, for Thomas is a man of the mind and not the body. It's where he feels most comfortable, where he feels at home.

The flames burn caverns into the candles. Wax pushes over the edges. I push my finger into the wax while it's still warm and pliant, leave my imprint.

We talk with intensity, drink wine until the bottle is empty, and the candles burn out, randomly like dying stars. The smaller ones, the tea lights, exhaust themselves until they're only wicks, and then die, too.

Our talk settles into silence, and then we burn out like the candles. It's how we spend our nights, Thomas and me. We sleep in the same bed now. Share intimate space as if we share our bodies, but we don't. We share other passions. Talk until we fall asleep, bodies touching just because they do, arm brushing against thigh, head against breast.

Chapter 22

There's more to story than the teller and her words. There's always the third. The observer changes the observed. Truth is mutable, and the listener acts upon the telling. I'd be remiss to leave you out of story.

*****

I trace the blue vein that runs up your arm like a river, the hollow of the inside of your elbow, the muscle of your forearm like hard-packed earth. You cringe with the delight of touch, and I, the traveller, continue the journey. You cringe again, and it amuses and delights me.

Body like geography, body like story.

Full of apple, full of story - we lie beside each other.

"Do you know of the prophet Mohammed?" I ask. "He said the three most precious things in the world are women, fragrant odours, and prayers. The prayer, now, that's debatable, but two out of three's not bad, especially for a prophet."

You smile, your hair aflame. I like to make you smile. Then you whisper my name as if I am a dream, *Michaela*. The sounds linger, and then are gone.

I think of the seagull that passes overhead on a blue summer day. You see its shadow fly across the ground, dark and swift, and it startles you. You take a moment to find your bearings, to think it through, and you realize that it is a bird.

You look up quickly, and it is gone.

I am that seagull.

The first time I saw you, we passed by each other on the street, your black dog at your heels like a shadow. We are passersby, and perhaps that is our bond. The invisible cord that ties us, strong and soft, like spider webs. We don't speak, don't yet exchange the look of lovers, that recognition in the eyes that is desire, the body memory of touch.

The snow and sleet have gone, but winter hangs in the air like a threat, and breath marks the air like exhaled souls. People gravitate to the street. They come out of their winter places, give up their rooms, their stairwells, the holes where they have hibernated. The man who shadowboxes, punching and jabbing at invisible ghosts; he's a shadow himself, but here, on the street, this night, he's the champ. Did you see him? Then the woman with the wool hat made from bright granny squares, herself pieced together like a mismatched quilt. She pushes a wire grocery bundle-buggy stuffed with plastic bags and bottles. She's happy, because spring has come, and she has places to go, and people to curse. She spits one at me, and I spit one back. Did she curse you too?

The runaways, skinny brash kids riding life like it's a fast train, always deal making, brokering transactions, drugs or blow-jobs, or both. I wonder if they ever had homes, or were born here, like a litter of mewling kittens scrounging for the teat of a scrawny cat. They'll cheat you, if you let them. Roll you, take your money, take your drugs, take your cigarettes, and leave you there, empty. I know. I have been them.

Then there are those who only visit. This is their fix. They stroll the street, take in a movie, take in a stage play, sip cappuccino at the trendy cafés and wine bars, and then leave, their urges satisfied. In the summer, they sit under the bright canopies that stretch over the patios. They talk literature, and stock market, and politics, and high-tech. They wear black and muted shades of brown and yellow, arrive in groupings divisible by two, always in pairs, couples or couples with couples, except for the men who come alone in their cars, circling the corners, cruising for sex.

The second time I see you, you sit on the street with your back to an old stone building. The dog sits beside you, and you rest against each other. Your hair is red like fire. The image seers me. I am careful not to catch your eye. Not yet, I'm not ready. You've unsettled me. That, in itself, is unusual, so you unsettle me twice. I'm Michaela, the girl who jumps out windows. Nothing unsettles me.

Chapter 23

I tip the jar. Pennies, nickels, dimes and quarters scatter across the kitchen table. Coins fall off the edge, and I dive under the table, surface with them clutched in my hand as if pearls from an oyster.

Nana has Pear on a diet. No more poutines and fried doughnuts, she scolds, placing a plate of celery sticks and cucumber slices and cottage cheese in front of him at the table.

"Anglais poop," Pear says when she leaves the room. He spits out the words, as if they are distasteful, both the English and the food.

Nana returns and puts a plate in front of me. It is piled high with chocolates and cookies and strawberries and bananas. She scolds me, too, but because I am skinny. "Eat," she says. "You need some fat on your bones."

Pear chuckles. We're comrades of sorts. We've both been scolded by Nana. It bonds us for the moment. I'm not angry with him anymore. Forgive him his refusal to say my mother's name. Anyway, I don't need him. Not Pear, or Nana, or the Aunties, or Mildred. The freedom is exhilarating. I feel invincible, as if I could fly, could jump from the window and soar. Defy gravity, in spite of past experience with the ground.

It's a pivotal discovery, this independence. I rely solely upon myself for the stories of my mother. I keep her alive in my mind. They can't stop me, can't enter there.

Pear eyes my plate, and sighs. The sigh escapes his mouth like a gentle wind. I slip Pear a chocolate, and he pops it whole into his mouth.

I help Pear eat the celery sticks and cucumbers slices, and he helps me eat the cookies and chocolate. Soon our plates are empty. Nana will be pleased with us. She likes empty plates. Now that we're finished, I stretch my arms wide across the tabletop so that all the coins are held within my reach. I pull the coins toward me, make a pile. I'm rich. I count the pennies, pulling them aside one by one with my finger.

"Pourquoi?" Pear asks, motioning toward the money.

"Because," I say.

We both have secrets.

"Pourquoi, Mee-kel-la?" Pear says, persistent.

I don't know why I tell him, what prompts truth and other times lies. I bend closer, so that we feel each other's breath upon our skin. We smell of chocolate, and cherry syrup, and conspiracy.

"The *sea*," I say earnestly.

We're so close to each other that the words fall from my lips and into his mouth, down his throat, into his belly. They come to rest inside of him like a sunken ship. How else can I explain the rest of my story?

Pear looks at me quizzically. He doesn't understand yet, even though the words sit inside of him, have already begun to work magic.

"What you *see*, Mee-kel-la?" Pear says.

"The *sea! Sea!*" I say. "I want to go to the *sea!*"

I move my arms expansively, denoting bigness. I make my eyes large, and open my mouth wide. Then I begin a new pantomime. Dive my hands downward like a dolphin might dive, dive deep to the very bottom of the sea, graze the floor with my fingertips, then spring back up, my arms giant waves.

I add sound to the drama, blow like the wind, puffing out my cheeks. I *am* the sea. Can't he see?

"Oooh-la-la," Pear says, his eyes brightening. "La *mer.*"

It's a new word for me. I roll it about my brain, try it on my tongue. I stretch out the "r", trill like Pear has done. There are waves in the sound.

I smile at Pear.

"Oui. La mer," I tell him.

I count the pennies again. I have lost my place, and must start all over. But that is fine, there is pleasure in the counting. Each penny brings me closer to the sea.

I want to give Pear pleasure, too, in exchange for the new word, so I count in French. *Un, deux, trois, quatre...*

Pear explodes in laughter. He pushes himself up from the chair, reaches his hand deep into his pocket. He takes out his little black change purse, squeezes it so that it opens like a fish's mouth. Coins spill out, and not only pennies. There is a silver dollar.

Pear puts the silver dollar into my palm. He folds my fingers over it, holds his hand there, as if making a pact.

"Bateau," Pear says.

"Bateau," I repeat seriously, then nod my head in agreement.

I can't decipher the word. I have no idea what Pear is saying, to what we have agreed, but it doesn't matter.

La mer is enough.

Chapter 24

I spot Pear before the others do, and whoop a warning cry to Nana. "The old Quebecois bat's hauling something big!" I squeal in delight. "Très, très, *très* big!"

"Don't call your grandfather names," Nana says. "What's the French fart got now?"

Pear pulls something on the trailer. It looks like a coffin, but no one has died. Not that I know of, anyway, but that doesn't mean much. They don't tell me anything around here, particularly about dead people. The dead are taboo. Forbidden fruit, if topics of conversation can be eaten. They mistake my thin bones, and pale skin, and fair hair as a fragility of body. And my few words, and preference for books, and propensity for running away, as a fragility of mind. Conversations stop when I enter the room. Words hang mid-sentence, mid-air, like lanterns strung across the patio. Sometimes the words are whispers, and other times they are loud and opinionated. But regardless, the voices stop, and the words swing tongue-tied in the silence.

"A corpse," I yell. "He's hauling a corpse."

The screen door slams, and I watch Nana march across the courtyard to the lions at the entrance. It's the only entrance to the estate. A stone fence surrounds the orchard and the garden and the manor. It's a barricade from the rest of the world, our own Great Wall of China.

Nana puts her hands on her hips. To an untrained observer, someone who doesn't know the strange dance that is Nana and Pear, she is angry. Her words say so, in tone and content, and her body confirms it. But things are not always what they seem.

Pear hauls mystery to her on the trailer.

Nana is excited. She won't admit it, not on the surface, where people think truth resides, like oil rests on water. But she's as excited as I am, as excited as Pear to show us what he has unearthed. Nevertheless, Nana will scold Pear that he's a silly old man, that he wastes his time and her money. And Pear will spit back that the Anglais have no imagination, no joie de vivre, that he and Quebec would be better off alone. And later, when they think I'm tucked in bed, a falsehood they hold as true because they did the tucking, I sneak out of bed, and watch Pear kiss Nana full on the lips, and call her his love, and she whispers, je t'aime.

The station wagon draws closer. I stand in the windowsill for a better look. From my birds-eye view, I see it's not the usual kind of coffin. It's too long and wide in the middle, and then I decide it must be a sarcophagus, and Pear has bought a mummy. It's not impossible that Pear has found a mummy at a garage sale. You never know what gathers dust in other people's cellars, Nana says. She speaks in such a way that makes me wonder what secrets gather dust in the locked cellar beneath our feet.

Pear pulls up to the stone gates. I jump from my windowsill, but not from my window. Land safely on the carpet, no broken bones. Dart from my room, down the maze of staircases, through the living room, past the mantle with the photograph of the pale man in the silver frame, push hard through the screen door so that it slaps behind me. For once, Nana doesn't yell at the sound.

I run around to the back of the station wagon before it stops, and stare in amazement at what Pear has hauled into the courtyard. It's bigger than it appeared from my windowsill.

Pear sticks his head out the window. His cheeks seem wider. I realize it's his smile. It washes broadly across his face, gives the appearance of immensity. "I keep promise," he shouts. "I bring Michaela bateau."

I jump up and down excitedly, and clap my hands, so that even Nana smiles. It's an unusual thing, my exuberance.

Chapter 25

Nana fusses with the picnic lunch, packs containers with cucumber and tomato sandwiches, hold-boiled eggs, strips of celery and carrots, a tub of spinach dip, potato salad, cabbage salad, bean salad, fits them perfectly, geometrically, into the picnic basket. Fills the jug with iced tea, and packs it in, too. Packs the remaining spaces with ice to keep the food from spoiling and the tea cold.

"La mer, m'enfant. Au'jour d'hui," Pear says, and then dances a silly little dance, a soft-shoe in his sock feet. He slips, regains his balance, almost nimbly.

"Don't deceive the child," Nana tells him.

Today, Pear doesn't care what Nana says and neither do I. He soft-shoes a circle around her, kisses her cheek, pats her bottom, pulls her hair. We're going to the sea.

"Why you say such evil things?" Pear teases her.

"It's a lake, not the ocean," Nana says.

Pear stops dancing. His mood changes suddenly, like the weather. I watch for other signs, worried. I don't want the weather to change. We're going to the sea. Pear has promised.

"Sea, ocean, lake, mer, it doesn't matter, Rosemary."

Pear tousles my hair so that it stands on end, sticks up

without the fur and comb, without the shift in electrical charge, negative to positive. All is well again. It will be a fair-weather day, after all.

I imitate his soft-shoe, a tap-less tap dance. Imitate his stumble, arms circling like I'm caught in a gale.

Pear roars at my pantomime, a huge wave of a roar.

Nana shakes her head, as if Pear and I are unredeemable. Her lips curl slightly in an almost-smile. "Go! Let me finish here," Nana says sternly, "or we will never get to the sea."

Pear grins at Nana's concession. The *sea*.

We're going to the sea.

Nana's face is flushed red, a tiny rosebud in the center of each cheek. I hadn't known that her name is Rosemary. It suits her, right now, this minute, if not at other times. Although perhaps it does, for then she is the thorn, and not the flower.

"Come, my little gypsy, we go check the boat," Pear says importantly, and we leave Rosemary to her packing.

The boat is freshly painted bright red and glistening white. An over-sized motor perches on the back as if it might fall off. The leather seats are polished with Armor-all, so the boat has that used car-dealer smell. I think I'm in a story, one of Nana's books, a great adventure, and we will sail the seven seas, or more, if there are more. Seven hardly seems enough, not for a world.

Pear takes my hand. His fingers are fat, and his wedding band squeezes the skin. So tightly, I think, that not even butter would slip it off. Pear, in response, squeezes my fingers, leads me around to the side of the boat. His palms are sweaty and warm.

"Ta-Da," he says, with grand showmanship, sweeping away an old blanket draped over the side.

The name of the boat spreads elegantly across the bow. The lettering is delicate, and I wonder how his fat fingers did it, how they managed to maneuver the curves and flourishes, to execute a paintbrush, like an artist instead of a junk collector. A garage sale addict. A garage sale-er. A garage sailor.

The Michaela.

I cannot be happier.

Chapter 26

As in many other things, you are not my first. I have told this sea-tale to Thomas before you.

"Who is Michaela?" Thomas interrupts the telling, candles burning on the table in front of us, their own constellation.

Thomas voices a question like it is supposed to be voiced, tone rising at the end of the sentence. He knows questions well. He's a scholar, after all, and thereby inquisitive. At least, when it comes to the details of a story, the workings of a thesis, the intersecting of facts and ideas.

It's the influence of the seminary. Church history. The Inquisition, and such. It's why I tell Thomas so little of my past. Keep my personal history personal for the most part.

"*The Mary*," I say. "Pear called the boat *The Mary*." The sleight of hand, the telling of the tale, the truth or lie. They ripen, like fruit. Skill takes practice, and so does deception.

Thomas looks at me oddly. He has heard what he has heard. It reminds me of Popeye and God, both claiming 'I am what I am.' I, too, am what I am. And also what I am not. And not what I am. And now Thomas, my Aquinas, claiming that he heard what he heard.

"Did you know the root of Mary is mer? The sea?" I say.

I pour Thomas wine. Nothing clouds the mind like wine. Rolls in like the fog. Just enough wine, and the mind is sharpened, the tongue quicker, less inhibited. And for most others, if not Thomas, the body, too. Too much wine, and the mind grows thick and useless. It's a fine balance, the pouring of wine, dependent upon purpose. I want Thomas to forget Michaela, and remember Mary.

"There are several words that trace their root to the same source. Maria means water. La mer, of course, is the French, maritime the Latin, and marine the English."

"Michaela."

Thomas says my name, as if practicing, the word unfamiliar on his tongue. The unfamiliarity is delicate, and oddly attractive. Not in itself, but in Thomas.

"Mary," I correct.

For once, Thomas ignores my attempts to circumvent. It is un-Thomas, this ignoring of facts and ideas. He reaches for my face, falls into me. His kiss is large and clumsy. He doesn't know what to do next, looks confused and willing. And so I do it for him. Help him to his feet, put him to bed, pull the blanket over him.

"Sleep, Thomas," I tell him.

He's drunk. I want more from Thomas. More *for* Thomas.

More than his regret. The fact surprises me.

It is so un-Michaela.

Chapter 27

The Aunties gather to see us off.

Mildred wears a straw sun hat with a pink chiffon scarf wound through it and tied in a big bow under her chin. A large swath of zinc oxide spreads across the bridge of her nose, and she smells of suntan lotion and insect spray. Sunglasses dangle from a chain around her neck and across her sinking breasts, two big ships on their way down. She sports a sailor shirt, white with a large navy collar, and gold trim and epaulettes, as if to say she's an officer, never the lowly fellow who swabs the deck. And she wears shorts, can you imagine? I stare at her bare legs, white and splotchy and fat.

The Aunties scurry into the house, more like anties than Aunties. They come out again, one by one, flap flap flap through the screen door, each carrying an item, and then back and forth again to get another, flap flap flap. Piece by piece, under Nana's direction, the items go into the car trunk. Picnic basket, lawn chairs stacked one on top of the other. Blankets and beach towels, beach bag with my bathing suit, sand pail and shovel to make a castle, and a blow-up sea-monster to wear around my waist.

Nana makes room for Pear's boat things. A paddle in

case the motor conks out, lifejackets, bailing can. The thought delights me, an emergency at sea. I jump up and down, and clap, unable to contain my excitement. Finally, Pear slams the trunk shut, and we all climb into the station wagon.

Pear looks at Nana expectantly. "Go, go," she says, and we wave goodbye to the Aunties, and they shout pleasantries, *Bon Voyage! Until we meet again! Have a good day! Don't take any wooden nickels, Michaela!* They are always saying that, don't take any wooden nickels, and I've yet to see a wooden nickel.

"How much longer?" I ask.

And then, after a hundred songs and a million miles, we're there.

"Ah, la mer, Mee-kel-a. It's beautiful, oui?"

I shake my head in wonder. *Yes, yes, it is beautiful!*

We cruise the parkway alongside the lake. I lean over Mildred's lap, reach for the window, roll it down. The water comes on a breeze, and I breathe it in deeply. Another smell comes too, and I don't know that it's fish and seaweed. It's perfume to me.

Pear maneuvers the station wagon so that we back down the boat ramp. He checks the rearview mirror, and then the side mirrors, turns the wheels, veers to the left. We hit the curb at the edge of the ramp and jerk. "Mary-Joseph-and-baby-Jesus" Mildred gasps.

I coach Pear. *Further to the right, a droit! A droit! A little further, there, straighten out the wheel, that's it, c'est bon, C'EST BON!*

Pear stops the station wagon, and I leap out before the ignition is off. I throw off my sandals, dance in the sand, pick up a seashell, stare into its cone. It's pink like the inside of an elephant's ear, pink like the morning sky. I hide the treasure in my pocket as if it's gypsy gold.

We unfasten the boat, lower it into the lake-sea, pull the boat around the dock as if leading a horse to the water, load the boat up, and then we're aboard. *Ships ahoy,* Pear shouts, and *th'ar she blows,* as if he sees a whale, and I look, and I see it! The back of a whale cuts an arch through the dark water, the black dorsal fin breaking the surface like a wave. It doesn't matter this is a lake and there are no whales. I have seen it.

The lake-sea is rocked by waves, and the rocking feels familiar. I think I remember it from another place. And then I *know* I remember it, and then I *do* remember it, and so it must be true, and so it *is* true.

The waves are soothing, like home. Not home in the sense of Nana and Pear's house, the big stone manor where I live, set in the midst of gardens and orchards and lawns. A stone fence to keep it all in, as if it might spill out, seep into the world like drainage and be gone. Not home like that. Home like this, a boat in the arms of the sea-lake.

Home that is a mother, my small body rocking against her breast.

*****

Waves slap against the hull, and I lean far over so the spray hits my face. *Faster, faster*, I yell at Pear. I stand on the seat, my small fingers clutching the top of the windshield.

Faster, faster, I say.

My mother pushes her body into the rocking, digs her feet into the floor. We laugh with glee at the motion, the chair's rockers slapping wildly against the hardwood.

"Michaela, sit!" Nana shouts. "You'll be thrown overboard!"

"Have mercy, Lord!" Mildred cries.

Mildred's voice shakes. She doesn't like the waves. I ignore them both, Nana and Mildred. Pretend not to hear their words, lost against the wind.

I watch the sails, silky and bright, and remember my mother's skirts, see them flapping about her ankles, as certain as memory.

"We should return to shore," Nana shouts.

The sky is dark grey now, and the water black. The wind is fierce, and the waves a meter high.

"Non," Pear says, deciding the best course is to stay the course, race the storm, beat it to the island.

Mildred wails. The wind grabs her hat, discards it to the

waves. The straw bonnet bobs among the waves, disappears then reappears, pink straps streaming behind it, and is lost at sea.

The boat pitches. Mildred eyes are crazed with fear.

"Get down," Nana cries. "Flat on the bottom."

Mildred hits the deck. Cowers on the floor. Nana reaches for me, but I jump aside, avoid her grasp. Climb up on the dashboard, lean over the windshield so that half of my body is above it. The wind blows my hair, and blows my body, but I'm skilled at the balancing game, let the storm buffet me, respond to the changes in the wind.

A dark funnel spins in the distance, winds gathering. The funnel skips across the water's surface, touches it, breaks free, touches it again. Twists and twirls, pattern of travel unpredictable. I screech with delight as the cyclone fools me, moves here, moves there, changes its route, dances closer.

It's then that I know I'm different from them, Mildred cowering on the bottom of the boat, saying her prayers, Nana huddled with her, Pear's face grim, hands in a death grip on the steering wheel. Waves wash over the bow, winds batter the boat, rains pelt us, and I'm ecstatic.

Lean further into the storm.

Chapter 28

Thomas fidgets. Moves his hand along the side of the coffee cup and around the handle. Lifts the cup to his mouth, sips a bit, but doesn't react to what he's sipped, the dregs of the pot. Even I spit it out, and Thomas likes it mild. *A bit of coffee with your hot water?* I've come to ask him in the mornings. It's a silly ritual, a kind of domesticity that I abhor, but I say it anyway, and I find it isn't abhorrent.

"You're late, better leave for the seminary," I tell him.

Thomas looks at the clock, but time doesn't register, or he doesn't care. That is new. Thomas cares about things like time.

"I'm sorry."

"You don't need to apologize for bagging class," I laugh. "Save it for the priest."

"I'm sorry," Thomas repeats and then, "I shouldn't have tried to kiss you."

My rage is sudden and big. Fills the crevices. The rush of adrenaline is familiar, an old friend, an old enemy. It's as much a part of me as my rake-thin body, my tiny breasts, my hair and skin, so damn moon-white. I fling Thomas's cup across the room. Scatter coffee across the floor, the grinds, black syrup like black ink.

"I'm sorry," Thomas says again.

He reaches for me. Thinks better of it, thinks better of temptation, picks up a cloth, bends to his knees, clears away the glass, wipes up the coffee stains.

Thomas on his knees, like a neutered monk. The sight enrages me even more, if that's possible, if rage is a matter of degree, a state of comparison - good, better, best. But I don't think so. The rage just is, all at once.

I find myself in the hallway, then out into the street. I don't remember the actual leaving, don't remember time and space, moving through them, moving through the door. I'm not wearing a coat. It's snowing, and I notice the cold, but the sensation is detached, as if it's not my cold, and I'm not in it.

I pace the street in front of the rooming house, flip the handles of parked cars along the curb. A van opens, and I feel under the front seat for a key to the ignition, under the visor, in the glove compartment. There's no key, so I crawl into the back seat, huddle under a wool blanket.

The adrenaline subsides, leaving me tired. When I awake, I'm cold and cramped, return to Thomas's empty room. He has left flowers for me on the table, a spilling bouquet of wildflowers. He's careful not to leave red roses, the traditional gift of lovers. He doesn't want me to misinterpret his intention. We are not lovers.

I wonder why Thomas is so confident I'll return that he leaves flowers. And then it hits me, like revelation. He compares me to himself, my leaving to his leaving. To go without planning, without gathering clothes and coat, without carefully packing a suitcase, is unfathomable. That I should leave without notice, without a forwarding address, telephone number, email, a million ways to contact each other, leave without thought and deliberation, midnight discussion, burning candles to the wick in the process, weighing the pros and the cons and reaching conclusions, is unthinkable.

I play the morning events in my mind, try to know my anger. Why it erupted like a storm at that point in the conversation. What triggered it. I think it's because Thomas equated a kiss with sin. That a kiss requires an apology, a confession. That kissing *me* is a matter for a priest. I imagine him, hidden in a dark booth, confessing to a kiss as if it is lewd, confessing to his desire for my body, as if it is sordid, both my body and his desire. Fingering his rosary and saying Hail Mary's in contrition. The only Mary he needs to finger is this Mary, if he feels such a need. I feel anger again, and then I know the precise source. I care what Thomas thinks. That is the trigger. It makes me even angrier that I care.

When he returns, Thomas brings me more gifts, his arms full. Take-out, and wine, and candles, a sky of candles. He serves me, formally, like a waiter. Refuses my help, sits me at the card table, lays out the dishes, spring rolls, shrimp and Chinese vegetables, egg noodles. Sets the candles among the plates, a Milky Way. Then we eat, and drink, and talk fervently into the night.

Chapter 29

"You're sprouting like a pea plant," Nana says.

It doesn't surprise me that she'd compare me to a plant, wishful thinking on her part. The fact of my growth makes the adults around me happy. They pat my head, as if I've done something to be commended, purposely grown three inches in two months, put my mind to it and did it, *grew*. If it were that easy, mind over matter, I'd be travelling the world and my mother would be alive.

After dinner, Pear makes me stand next to the doorframe in the kitchen. He takes a knife and scratches a notch in the wood. There are other marks on the doorframe, old knife scratches. I run away into the parlour to escape Pear and his notches. I am just tall enough that my fingers touch the photo frame on the mantle, the one with the silver frame and the crack across the glass. I slip my middle finger around the corner, pull the frame closer. The picture falls into my hands, and I catch it. Place the frame under my shirt. It's cold against my skin.

I sneak into Nana's room. Put the photo on the floor so that the man with the corn-yellow hair and moon-white skin stares out at me. I examine his face, touch it with my fingertips.

Touch my own face, my nose, my cheeks, like a blind man feeling an image, making it reappear in his imagination.

Then I go to Nana's dresser. Everything is orderly. Nana is orderly. A brush set, comb and fancy brush and a hand mirror. Set out neatly, as if for show alone, and I wonder if she uses it, and if not, what is its use.

I take the mirror, plop down on the floor, look at myself, look at the man in the frame, look at myself again, look at the man. His eyes are pale blue.

"You're the spitting image of him, Michaela."

Nana's voice makes me jump.

"Sometimes I think you *are* him, and he is a boy again."

If it's a spitting image she wants, then I'll give it to her, and I spit in her direction. Then I spit at the photo. I'm angry to have been discovered looking at the man in the frame, angry that Nana would speak these lies to me.

I throw the mirror, and it clatters across the floor, another crack in another glass.

Chapter 30

Thomas says it's original detail that leads scholars to the truth in the telling. Scholars un-layer the Gospel narratives to find the real events and sayings of the historical Jesus. "Scholarship is like stripping paint and varnish off an old table to get to the bare wood," he says. "If you strip them away, you're left with the original wood. Likewise, if you strip away the untruths, the layers of history, the hidden agendas of the particular time of the telling, monk-scribes adding their personal take, strip away the commentary, you're left with historical fact."

Thomas is big on the historical. It leads to a lively disagreement about the validity of truth. Truth is nothing outside context, I say. Truth is everything, he insists, and there can only be one truth, regardless of context.

"What if you strip everything away and there's nothing left?" I counter. "What if everything you thought was true, believed to be fact, proves to be false? When it is all said and done, does it really matter? Isn't the story itself worth something? What if what you're stripping away has more value than what you reveal?"

"There's always something left," Thomas says, "and the truth is always worth it."

He believes things like that, Thomas. The clichés. *The truth is always worth it.* I expect him next to say something like the truth will set you free.

That night, Thomas's breathing is rhythmic. I can hear it, feel it against my skin. In his sleep, Thomas pulls me closer, his arm around my waist, his hand slipped under my shirt, his body cradled around my back, his face pressed into the crook of my neck. A candle hisses a final protest, and then we are left to the dark.

PART TWO

The Story within the Story

Chapter 31

I've learned a lot about the Rom throughout the years. I know that they've been persecuted, home-camps torched, burnt to the ground, jeering crowds forcing them to move again, the open road not always a choice. Know that their name is an ironic accident of language, since they roam the earth. That they speak Romani, an oral language. A written language holds no value to them, since the story changes with each telling. It's the present moment that is true, the present telling.

I know that the word Rom has no root in the word Romania, although many Rom live there. Language, it seems, is full of accidents. The Rom lineage, the open road, is retraced to India. It's a modern story, told by linguists, trotting out proof in words common to both Hindi and Romani. The collaboration for the linguist's story is in the body, the evidence in the dark skin, almost blue, the dark hair, the dark eyes. I know *all this* about the Rom and her way of life.

About Nadja.

*****

It takes the dancer years of dancing, years of travelling, to be able to express journey with her body. To find this talent in one so young, Nadja must surely be the reincarnation of a great gypsy from the past, the storytellers say with the irrefutable authority of story. She must surely have danced in the famous flamenco cafés in Spain, long before her thirteen years, or in India centuries ago, sari-dressed and bare-footed, golden bells about her ankles. And they tell the one story and then the other, India and Spain, right after each other, both vividly true.

Word of Nadja's beauty has travelled afar, in the way that stories travel, on a gust of wind along the open road. The storytellers speak as if they've seen her themselves, as if the story has originated with them and not the wind. They gild the telling with shiny words almost as pretty as Nadja. They tell how her hair is jet-black and thick like a horse's mane, how she wears it loose, setting her apart from the other girls, their hair tied into braids. How she doesn't yet wear a kerchief knotted at the back of her head in the tradition of married women, for she's not married. How her skin is the colour of a walnut, her eyes jade green and her lips scarlet red. How her dowry of gold is woven through her hair, and hangs from her neck, gold coins drilled and strung and worn as necklaces, thick gold hoops through her ears, and around her wrists.

They tell how she holds the knowledge of her beauty in her carriage, in the way she moves, a haughtiness in her, back straight, head high, a sway to her hips, the *baile*, the dance, present even in her walk. The storytellers don't stop there, but speak of another beauty. How Nadja's dancing arouses the passion of the traveller's stories, the sadness of those who have suffered much along the journey, the freedom of the long road, the independence that is the gypsy's heartbeat.

Chapter 32

Nadja thinks she's a princess, an old woman says, sitting on a stump and listening to the stories. She chews on the words, spits them out along with her tobacco. Then she smiles, gaptoothed, her leather skin wrinkling, deep troughs in her face. She smiles because she remembers her own princess days. Every gypsy is a princess, especially at thirteen, and every gypsy is royalty, if only of her own story.

This is the courtyard of Nicu's family. He's the man that Nadja will marry, if the bartering goes as planned, if the words and the promises and the hyperbole bear fruit. Nicu is older than Nadja, fourteen, the eldest son of the *bulibasha*, the local Rom leader. He'll be leader himself someday, inherit the crown, and Nadja, too. She'll become wife of the *bulibasha*, a gypsy queen instead of a gypsy princess.

Nicu is handsome, his eyes alive and laughing. His skin is as dark as Nadja's, his hair oddly out of step with time, thick and black, bangs swept across his forehead, just above his eyebrows, like a wave about to break.

Nicu's house is all for show and not for living. The rooms are big with expensive wool carpeting, and fine furniture, and velvet wallpaper, and fancy baseboards. There are gilt lamps on gilt tables, and stone statues of maidens, and curved staircases with wrought iron, and oil paintings of galloping horses.

For guests, Nicu's father says, with a flourish of his hand that takes in the villa, and the gypsies understand what he means. No gypsy would live in such a house, and no gypsy is ever a guest. Guests are *gadje*, and gypsies are family. Here, behind the house - this is where the living happens. There are open fires where the old women still cook, and tubs where they still wash their clothes by hand, clotheslines spread out between rusty poles. There are folding card chairs where the men sit and talk and smoke, a chicken or two scratching in the ground, a mangy dog sniffing for scraps.

Nadja's little sisters look upon her with envy. They play at the outer edge of the circle, where the Rom have gathered in the open air. The Rom prefer the open air to houses, prefer the backyard to rooms like Nana's parlour, carved-feet sofas and carved-back chairs, mantle carefully lined with photos, silent history held on a shelf instead of a spoken history held in the story.

The little sisters peer through the legs of the men, around the skirts of the women. They think they see Nadja, starting the slow swirl of the flamenco. Think they see her bare feet, the balls pressing into the grass. Practice the movements, twirl about the outer rim of the circle, like moons to a planet. They pretend they are Nadja. Little girls imitating big girls. It's the same everywhere.

Nadja stands at the inner edge of the circle. She waits for the Rom to stop their haggling, their bragging, their eating, their drinking. She pulls herself taller, pulls up through her neck and back, holds arrogance in her body. Conversation falls away, bit by bit, like leaves scattered by the autumn wind. Still Nadja doesn't move, even when silence hangs over them.

Someone shouts dance! dance! and others take up the call. A gypsy claps his palm with the fingers, crosses his right hand over his body to hit his left hand, makes a sharp piercing sound. The other Rom join in. Most clap, too, although some snap their fingers, and others rap the tabletops. The guitarist drops his hands, begins to play.

Now the moment is right.

Nadja dances in the old style. Subdues her steps, doesn't draw attention to her feet. Her arms, her hands, her hips, her torso perform the dance, draw you into it. She doesn't know where this comes from, she didn't learn it. It's where she is led.

Maybe it's true that she is reincarnated. Maybe a ghost moves through her. Maybe ghosts. Maybe the dancer's body is the repository of gypsy history, the record of where the Rom have travelled, which roads they have taken. India, and Greece, and Imperial Rome, and Persia and Turkey; echoes of synagogue chants, and calls to prayer from mosque minarets, and the castanets of Cadiz dancers, and the cry of Moorish warriors.

It has been a long journey, and an ancient one.

This is Nadja's dance.

Chapter 33

I've seen the photo.

Two photos actually, the wedding photo and the dowry photo, the *čeiz*. They're both prized to Rom families, but if you had to choose one, taking sudden flight, you'd choose the *čeiz*, hands down. In the *čeiz*, there is Nadja, decked out in white like a virgin bride, a white pillbox hat on her head that must have belonged to someone else before her. She sits there, prim and proper, on the bed, propped up for a photo shoot, surrounded by dowry. There's a small smile on her face, and she looks directly at the camera, unafraid of it. I imagine she sees me at the other end, further down the road, and maybe she does, looks straight at me.

Nadja is young. A young girl playing dress-up, if this were another culture, another place. As if she puts on her mother's clothes, tries on the role of woman, and then takes the clothes off, folds them up and puts them away in the chest for a later time.

In the second photo, the wedding picture, Nadja and Nicu stand side by side, rather formally. They look at the camera and not each other. They're dressed in civilian clothes, as if going to City Hall. And that is where they go. City Hall for the paperwork - the real wedding, the Rom wedding, is a private affair between man and woman, between the bed sheets.

I don't know what happened to the photos. After the rocking slowed down, finally stopped, like a creek icing over. My sitting there, in her lap, waiting for the morning, not knowing if morning would ever come.

Nana and Pear must have thrown them out.

Chapter 34

On the night of Nadja's wedding, the old women inspected her. They clucked excessively, pointed out her good parts. Pointed at the thick bushy hair at the top of her legs - *that is good*, they nodded and clucked in agreement. The hair shows she's fertile and healthy and all Rom. They tried to poke further. Nadja pushed away their hands, won't let them between her legs to feel for her virginity.

Nicu's grandmother grins at Nadja, flashing gold. *No matter*, she says. *We'll wait for the blood on the bed sheets.* She pats Nadja's abdomen, leaves both hands there, listening through the palms. Drops her hands suddenly, then flutters her fingers for Nadja to climb into a washtub.

The old woman is beautiful to the gypsies - for her teeth, and for her curses. The gold in her mouth reminds the other Rom with her every word, every smile, that she's the widowed wife of a *bulibasha*. Her curses, it is said, can kill with her glance alone. The Rom show their admiration in the wordless whispers of their body. The way they defer to her, let her enter and leave a room first, watch for the flutters of her hand to carry out her wishes, wait until she has spoken before they pass judgement, wait until she has sat in the best chair before they sit.

She no longer serves meals unless she wants to serve them, and the fattest pieces of meat are reserved for her plate. And it's not just the women, but the men, too. She sits with the men often now. Sits with them around the tables during the day while the other women work, while the other women keep the men's mugs full and the tobacco butts swept away from their feet. She drinks the same thick black coffee-syrup as the men, smokes the same hand-rolled cigarettes and cigarillos, flicks the butts. Spits out her stories and her opinions and her curse words, and guffaws just as loudly. Sits with her legs wide apart, her skirt hem over her knees so the dark cloth is spread taut like a tent. She no longer bleeds like the younger women and is treated with the respect of a man.

With the agreement of marriage, words of honour spoken among gypsies, Nadja has become communal property and her virginity a communal matter. Nicu senses the difference, too. There is no more lovemaking in the back seat of an old car in an old car graveyard, no more mad groping behind corners when no one is looking. He spends his time with the men, playing cards and smoking tobacco, and talking, always talking. The men grin at Nicu and poke him in jest, slap his back and pretend to grab his balls. They make jokes about his manhood, about his manliness, pass knowing looks amongst themselves about his wedding night. Offer to take his place, if he's not up to the task with his young wife.

A Rom woman's life is hard and the young wives, their lives are the hardest of all. They leave their families and move into the homes and caravans and tents of their husband's family. They perform the household chores. They bear babies year after year, but if the young wives live long enough, work hard enough, complain little enough, then they will become mothers of sons of marrying age, and then old women. They'll inspect the brand new wives, wash and bathe them for their wedding night, pat them dry with thick towels, rub their bodies with sweet oils and thick creams, dress them in the silk for their wedding nights, and then inspect the wedding sheets for virgin blood.

Chapter 35

The old women hover outside the door. They listen closely for sounds from the bedroom, erupt in anger when their listening is disrupted. One slaps a toddler sharply across the back of his legs for running around the coffee table. Another slaps a little girl across the top of her head for asking for water. They scold the offending young mother by pointing fingers in her direction, shooing her and her brood into the backyard with the chickens.

The old women listen for the sounds of lovemaking, the thump-thump-thump of the bedsprings, the sink of the bed into silence, the marriage consummated. They listen for Nadja's sharp scream, like the yelp of a dog, her hymen broken, the virgin skin torn, bloodying the bed sheets. They listen for Nicu's sigh, his collapse into Nadja when he's spent. They listen for all of that.

The gypsy men, friskier than usual, tease their gypsy women. They pat their women's bottoms, and peacock-prance for them, as if too big for their britches and they probably are, thoughts of Nicu and Nadja in the other room. They boast that the wait of the old women will be a long one. Not because Nicu doesn't know where to put it, fumbles away in the bedroom, but because he'll put it several times, all through the night.

That the future *bulibasha* will rise to the occasion like the gypsy royalty that he is, as did his father before him on his own wedding night. That the old women might as well put away their spells for testing virgin blood until morning, and the gypsy mothers and daughters-in-law put away the food and drink. Send home the music makers and the dancers, for the celebration could wait until Nicu was finally done.

*****

Nadja and Nicu sit at the edge of their wedding bed. They look at each other awkwardly. You wouldn't know that they're already married, in the legal sense, the solemn trip to City Hall made last week, where they signed the official papers in front of the judge, Nicu's uncle and father, the witnesses. The real wedding, in the eyes of the Rom, would happen in this bedroom. Would happen when Nadja and Nicu became man and wife, when the bed sheets showed it and the old women declared it by examining the bloom of the blood on the bed sheet.

You wouldn't know that they had made love many times in the past, that they weren't shy around each other or their bodies. You couldn't tell by looking at them, perched on the edge of their bed, nervously twisting their hands, that they knew exactly how to please each other. That Nadja's fingertip on Nicu's nipple could make parts untouched swell, that Nicu's tongue against Nadja's inner thigh could make her groan and arch her back. The slower the lovemaking, the greater the desire, the greater the pleasure. These are not things you learn on your wedding night.

Nadja's stomach is queasy. She's been retching for more than a month now, but has managed to hide the illness from her mother. Either that, or her mother decided not to notice, the marriage contract signed and sealed, the delivery of the virgin goods all that remains. If truth be known, Nadja's mother loves Nadja. Can't bear to think what will become of her daughter if she isn't a virgin and then is pregnant. What mother could bear it? The Rom will scorn Nadja, declare the marriage null and void. She'll be a teenage mother with no husband to support her, and no gypsy man would ever marry her.

Some young unmarried gypsy mothers sell pencils and their bodies on the street corners to live – both at the same price – sometimes a bargain, two for the price of one. They put their bastard children to work, begging from *gadjo*, foreigners.

Some young unmarried gypsy mothers maim their bastard children to invoke pity. Cut off a limb, or blind an eye, or knife-scar a cheek to make the greatest gain from the begging. An injured beggar-child garners more coins than a whole-bodied one.

It's easier for Nadja's mother to ignore Nadja's quick exits, the retching, her daughter's pale face, the loss of appetite for some foods, her cravings for new foods. To leave the outcome to fortune, good or bad, than to set in motion the worse.

Chapter 36

"Did you get it?" Nadja asks.

Nicu nods, motions towards the chair.

Nadja kisses him, and for a moment it's as if they are in the old car again. He returns the kiss, and they fall into the sheets, talcum powder rising like dust around them. Nicu coughs, and Nadja squeals, pulling a plastic rose from beneath her back.

The old women have scattered the bed with the plastic roses. Nadja would have preferred wildflowers. The talcum powder is stifling. The room smells stale, as if the windows went unopened for years. She wonders about the old women and their dreams. What the plastic roses mean to them, the talcum powder, the oils and creams, the negligee they have dressed her in, the way they have brushed her hair, like she is a gypsy doll. Nadja doesn't know enough about being a young gypsy wife yet, doesn't understand that the old women give her this night before the drudgery of her daily life begins. It's the best they can do, and it comes from their own dreams, the faded memories of their own wedding day, what they wish it had been, and so make it now.

"Let me see," Nadja says.

Nicu lifts the chair cushion, brings back a bag, hands it to her. Nadja feels a rush of love for him. It's a love that only a Rom can know for another, for things gypsy. The detail of the planning, the delicacy of execution, the risk he takes for her, the stakes of the scam. It is love like adrenaline.

She has no idea how he did it, old women bustling about like flies, fixing this, rearranging that. How he slipped the bag under the cushion without being seen, without being caught red-handed, the blood on his hands so to speak. Whether he'd encountered a gypsy grandmother, what he said to her, how he had maneuvered himself out of danger, oil-slippery and cloying. Flattering the old woman, flirting with her, complimenting the way she looked that day, the way she had scattered plastic flowers across the bed, talcum powder on the sheets, how she knew what a future *bulibasha* would like.

Nicu and Nadja had first planned to wring the neck of a chicken, slit its throat, drain the blood into a can, hide the remains, and if the remains were found, blame the death on a coyote, or a roaming cat. But chicken blood was unreliable, wouldn't fool the old women, although it might fool a younger woman less experienced.

Pig's blood was better. It congealed almost the same as virgin blood when the bed sheet was spread across the kitchen table, plum brandy sprinkled on the stain. They wouldn't be the first to try such a scam. Nadja might have used pig's blood. It was simple enough, a trip to the butcher in a neighbouring town, spiriting a small vial into the bedroom, emptying it onto the bed sheets. But the stakes are immense. If she's to pull off a scam, she has to be smarter, more gypsy, than the old women, and in particular, Nicu's grandmother.

Nadja pulls the bed sheet from the plastic bag. She looks at the sheet on the bed, compares the two. The fabric's the same - shiny taffeta the old women reserve for weddings - bed linens that get scrubbed and put away until marrying season comes round again. She knits her thick dark eyebrows together, holds the bed sheets side by side, scrutinizes them. The linens aren't the identical shade of white. The one from the bag is faded. It has endured more wedding nights and next-day beatings at the scrub-boards of the young wives, bleached longer by the sun on the clothesline, and whipped harder by the wind.

But it'll have to do.

"Whose blood is it?" Nadja asks.

She's not certain why she wants to know. She tells herself it is to ensure every detail is in order. Maybe she's jealous.

"Lena," Nicu says.

The perfect choice, Nadja knows.

She's felt Lena's envy.

It would have been easy for Nicu to take Lena by the hand, lead her through the darkness to the abandoned trailers. Lie her on the mattress, on the wedding sheet, put there for this purpose, the shadows dim in the trailer.

"Do you think she'll tell?" Nicu asks.

Nadja shakes her head. Lena wouldn't be such a fool. Instead, she'll scheme her own scam when the time comes.

They pull off the clean sheet from the bed, flatten it, place it into the bag, slip the bag back beneath the chair cushion. "We can't open the door yet for the inspection," Nadja says. "This blood is dry. We'll need to wait until morning, and we should make the sheet look slept in."

So the old women must listen and wait, while the men toast the stamina of their future *bulibasha*, and the young wives fill their glasses. And the Rom children play in the courtyard and fall asleep in the moonlight, while Nadja and Nicu make sweet love in their wedding bed on a bed sheet that is stained with virgin blood.

Chapter 37

The young wives pull Nadja from the crowd that is gathering, Rom stirring from their places of sleep. They consider Nadja one of their own now, even though the old women must still officially declare it. They think of Nadja as a sister, even though she marries into Nicu's family, the *bulibasha's* first and only daughter-in-law. But the gypsy family is large, and everyone is related somehow, and so Nadja is one of them.

For the first time, the young wives have Nadja to themselves. The celebration starts in earnest in an hour or so, and soon they'll be occupied serving their men. The small window of time for frivolity is unusual, and they snatch it, especially now that they've been shooed from the kitchen for the inspection of the bed sheets. Nadja is the wife of the future *bulibasha*, and they compete for her attention, work to curry her favour, and why not? It's expedient of them to do so, gypsy-smart. It's a long life, the gypsy life, and nothing is forgotten. Their children will grow and marry, and have children themselves, and the old ones will die, and the young wives will someday be old women, and Nadja will be the most powerful among them.

The food and drinks are ready and the long dinner

table set. The smaller children's table is ready, too, although the urchins can take care of themselves. They're gypsies, after all. They'll scrounge like puppy dogs, grab what they want from this plate and that plate, and then run into the courtyard to eat. Imitate their elders with their loud boisterous play, tease each other, practice one-upmanship, scam the best scraps from the dinner table away from the hands of their playmates, come back for more, and begin the game again.

The young wives pull at Nadja, pull her by the hands, pull at her skirts. Pull her into a back room, push down on her shoulders so that she sits at a fold-up card table. Stretch her arms across the card table, lie her palms flat on the tabletop, paint elaborate patterns with henna on Nadja's hands.

Nadja is grateful for the distraction. The chatter settles the fluttering in the belly, the nervousness at the ritual the old women perform in the kitchen, the nausea of the morning sickness. She thinks she feels a kick, but surely it is too soon for kicking. If she stays still, sits in this chair, stays quiet, she thinks she can control her stomach, won't have to escape from the room to retch. The young wives fuss with her hair. One takes a bright kerchief, places it on Nadja's head, knots the cloth behind Nadja's neck. It is an outward sign of marriage, how Nadja will be expected to wear her kerchief from this time onward. Back-tied.

Sounds erupt from the kitchen, voices and shuffling, the beginnings of celebration. The tests are done, the plum brandy poured, the blood congealed, the pattern pored over and pondered. With quick jabs of their fingers, the old women have pointed out the blood curls, discussed it amongst themselves, have reached a verdict.

"A perfect bloom," they say, except Nicu's grandmother, who says nothing. But it's true, the bloodstain is exquisite, forms the shape of the flower, a cherry blossom, petals rounded, for all to see.

The gypsies pull Nadja into the kitchen, push husband and wife side by side so that they press against each other in the crowded room. *They'll make beautiful babies together*, someone shouts. Others hoot their agreement and raise their glasses. The men nudge each other, thinking of sex, and the women nudge each other, thinking of beautiful babies, and the young wives look wistful, and glance at their husbands, and know that their babies will never be so beautiful as those of Nicu and Nadja.

And how could they not think that way?

Nicu has been blessed with walnut-skin, if you can call it being blessed and not just the luck of the genes, how the cards are dealt. His face is smooth and without blemish, no pocks or warts or ugly moles. His hair is jet-black, and falls over his eyes in a way that makes him boyish, although he has proved himself to be a man. His body and legs are strong and muscled, and the gypsy women can only imagine how well he is hung, except for Lena, and she's not saying. Nicu's smile is quick to erupt, spreads across his face. He has all his teeth, and best of all, they are pearly white, not stained yellow like the other gypsy men, sucking on their cigarillos, chewing and spitting tobacco, teeth blackened and decayed from stuffing too much Turkish toffee into their mouths.

And Nadja, well Nadja.

Her babies will be olive-skinned, and dark-haired, and they'll have jade eyes, and pudgy faces, and when they grow up, they'll have high cheekbones, and willowy bodies, and firm ample bosoms if they are girls. Like their mother, they'll have the gift of dance in their bodies.

Chapter 38

The Rom men grab the bed sheet, tear it away from the kitchen table, hold it above their heads, trail it behind them like a flag or pennant. Now *their* rituals will begin, the manly traditions. They are done with the old women, and plum brandy, and declarations. They are done with wives, and the waiting, and the dowry bargaining, and the *ceiz*, and the wedding night. They'll leave the women to the kitchen, and to the children, and to their own rituals, and gossip and stories.

The men sweep Nicu into the courtyard. Raise him up, drop him into the back seat of an old Cadillac convertible, the kind auto manufacturers used to make, when gas was cheap, and cars were long and sleek, and had fins that flared at the back like two sharks swimming side by side.

The Cadillac leads the parade through the narrow streets of the small village. The Rom men follow in their big outdated cars, honking horns, and whooping and hollering, squares of bed sheet flapping in the wind, tied to their radio antenna and from their mirrors, along with the crucifixes and plastic dice. When the parade winds its way back, it's twice as long as when it started, gaining Rom and even *gadjo* along the way.

Finally, the men are ready for the noonday meal. They have toiled hard, for whooping and hollering is never easy. At sounds from the courtyard of squealing, and revving, and honking, and hollering, the gypsy women rush to remove lids off steaming plates. They lay food the length of the long banquet table, a variety of dishes. Warm breads and spreads, platters of chicken legs and chicken breasts, thick slices of pork and beef, chunks of fat left on for those who like the taste of fat. Rice dishes and noodle dishes and goulash dishes, stews and soups so thick that they can be ladled or cut, creams and gravies and jellies to pour over foods, sweets and cakes and pastries, sprinkled with icings and powders and sugars.

Today is a day of show. A day to make banquet of food and drink, but also to make banquet of prestige and wealth. To display the *bulibasha's* riches for all to see, spread them out, like food on the table, for a gypsy's riches are measured not only in gold, but in friends, and family, and gypsy generosity. And in the end, when all is told and done, riches are measured by the stories they generate. How far the stories travel, and how long the stories live.

The *bulibasha* stands at the head of the table, raises his glass, toasts everyone individually and collectively, wild rambling poetic toasts. He toasts the bride and groom, raises glasses to their fertility, to their future offspring. Toasts the old women, and then his own mother, Nicu's grandmother. Toasts his wife, the love of his gypsy life, the beloved mother of his four sons, the blessed mother of Nicu, the future *bulibasha*. Toasts the virgins and their would-be suitors. Toasts his dead gypsy father. Toasts the Rom wherever they are, and wherever they travel, toasts the open road, and toasts the winding story.

Wineglasses and then carafes are emptied and refilled, and still the toasts are not done. Continue throughout the banquet until everyone in attendance and some who aren't have been toasted. Glasses clink, cutlery tinkling against crystal. Nicu and Nadja answer the call, stand to kiss, a small kiss that doesn't stop the clinking, or satisfy the gypsies. So they stand again, kiss again, better this time, longer and more passionate, a show like any other gypsy show, a flaunting of the story, and the Rom cheer.

The music begins, and Nadja and Nicu are the first dance. There is a hush, and the gypsies fall silent. They feel the flamenco in the way Nadja holds her body, and nostalgia for all things Rom.

Nadja is dressed in a traditional bridal gown. The train of the gown is longer than the banquet table, yards of silk flowing from Nadja's back. A *gadjo* eager for gypsy business is the first to pin cash to the dress. The Rom cheer, and laugh, and raise their glasses. Pin money of their own. Making sure the other gypsies, and the *bulibasha*, and the *bulibasha's* son, their future gypsy leader, are watching. Each outdoes the other, bigger denominations, more bills, never in a quiet moment, but with great fanfare, until the train of the wedding dress is now pinned full of money, the skirt, too, and then there is still more money, and Nadja takes off her shoe. The toe is stuffed with cash, another gypsy tradition, a Rom variation of the Cinderella tale.

The music is loud, and now the dance floor full. Finally, finally, Nadja is able to steal a moment for herself, slip through the side archway of the large hall. She glides through the back paths of the courtyard, the train folded over her arm, the shoe clasped in her hand. A bill falls, and she doesn't bother to pick it up. There are enough of them.

A few fires have been stoked in the old oil drums. Gypsies gather around them, smoking and swapping stories. They don't think it odd that Nadja takes a stroll in her wedding dress, money dangling from her. She's Rom, after all, and Rom prefer the open air.

Nadja comes to the place of the broken trailers, a place of abandoned gypsy dreams. Climbs into the old car where she and Nicu first made love. Sits there for awhile, and thinks of the past few days. Thinks of her life so far. For a reason she can't define, closer to intuition than anything else, she takes money from the shoe. Unpins some of the money from her train, fifties and hundreds. Rolls the bills together, climbs out of the car, unlatches the hood, her henna hands stained with rust and dirt. Stashes the money in the car. Then traces her path back towards the wedding celebration.

In the courtyard, Nicu's grandmother steps out of the shadows.

Blocks Nadja's way.

The old woman is quick, and Nadja hadn't expected her.

"*If* you were a virgin on your wedding day," the old woman grins widely, flashes gold, "Your firstborn will be all gypsy, swarthy and dark like Nicu. And if you were *not* a virgin on your wedding day, may that brat in your belly be as pale as the moon, as yellow as straw, the colour of *gadjo*."

Nadja reaches for her stomach, her Cinderella shoe clattering to the cobblestone. She is too late to stop what has been put in motion, knows a curse when she hears it, as any gypsy does.

Chapter 39

Nadja grows fat. Her belly bulges and her feet swell. She sweeps the courtyard with a straw broom, stops to watch a spider sitting in a web. It, too, is fat, the size of her thumbnail, all body. Nada doesn't brush the web away, leaves the spider alone.

The baby's dropped. That's what the other gypsy women say, watching Nadja like she is the spider in the spider web. They wait, make small wagers. Coins pass hands, bits of jewellery, unwanted chores, another day gone by that Nadja hasn't given birth. They marvel amongst themselves, how fat Nadja is. Dish her extra helpings of food, watch the baby fall day by day, surely ready to tumble out by now. They count the months, seven since the wedding, but do not count them aloud. She is, after all, Nadja. The wife of the future *bulibasha*, and the bloom of the blood was virgin.

There is only so long that Nadja can hold back her baby, stop her baby from being born. The pains come, and she tries to wish them away, to make the baby behave and stay put inside of her. But the baby's not a child to behave by nature, and a gypsy girl is born, right there in the courtyard, the spider watching.

The young wives gather around, then run for the old women. They pick Nadja up in their arms, her women's blood staining the cobblestones. They carry Nadja and the infant, still joined to the umbilical cord, to a back room away from the men, for the birth of babies is a matter for women. It's only then that someone washes away the blood that stains the infant, washes away the gypsy. Reveals a child the colour of the moon, the colour of straw, the colour of cheese. Tufts of hair the colour of corn silk.

No one utters a word.

Not the old women, or the young wives pressed flat against the walls of the tiny back room. Not even the baby makes a sound. Nadja thinks the baby is stillborn, tries to pull herself up.

It would be better if the child dies before she sucks a single breath, the gypsies think. *This is not the baby of Nicu.* They don't bother to clear away the mucus from her mouth, don't bother to slap her bottom. But the baby sucks breath into her tiny lungs, fills them up like little balloons. Cries without the prompting of the slap, makes a sound pale and weak like her color.

Nadja reaches towards the thin wail of a sound, and the old women put the baby in her arms. They're too dumbfounded to think straight, to do anything else, although Nicu's grandmother thinks to smile.

The baby suckles, her head small and moon-like against Nadja's breast. The tug is strong for such a pale rag of a thing. Maybe there's a bit of the moon in her after all, for the tugs are tidal pulls, and the child brings down milk. Drinks as if she knows famine is just around the bend in the road. Feasts while she can, and in that way, she's undeniably gypsy.

The old women try to take the infant from Nadja's arms, but the baby won't let go, and neither will her mother. Nadja snarls, like a mad dog.

"You've lost blood," they tell her. "You're weak, and you need sleep, and you're delirious. Give us the child, and we'll clean her, rub her with oils, bind her tightly in a gypsy shawl, keep her safe from bad fortune, and return her to your breast."

Nicu's grandmother hangs in the background like a picture. She's always there, and when Nadja drifts off, the old woman sits at the edge of her dreams. She whispers to Nadja, a flash of gold as blinding as the sun.

"There is a way," she says, and leaves it at that, waits the curse to play itself out.

The murmurs of the gypsy women have reached their men, but no one speaks the words to Nicu, the gypsy men silent when he sits in the courtyard with them. Their storytelling stops, and the preposterous claims, and the boisterous games, and the backslapping, and ball grabbing. The Rom look to the ground, look away, busy themselves rolling tobacco, sucking nicotine, flicking the butts further and further afield. The young wives run to sweep butts up, happy for the chance to keep gypsy life the way it should be, to keep everything and everybody in their proper order.

One by one, the men escape the courtyard to attend business in the next village, over the ridge of hills, anywhere but here, with Nicu. A future *bulibasha* whose wife has given herself to another, and after the wedding night, *for didn't they all see the bloom of the blood on the bed sheet?* It must have been a foreigner passing through the village. A Dutchman or an American for how else could you explain the *gadjo* hair, the *gadjo* skin? A child the colour of the moon, the colour of straw, the colour of cheese. Tufts of hair the colour of corn silk.

*****

Nicu wonders if Nadja is dead.

He feels a stab of panic, but lets the panic settle. Nadja can't be dead, or the child. There are no wails, no running for the priest. Nicu now wonders if the child is ill. Born sickly, without all her parts, or too many of them. Four fingers, or six. Born without a leg, or with a leg that dangles uselessly. Born with eyes that don't see, or ears that don't hear, or a head that is misshapen and squat and stupid. What else can it be? At the slightest excuse to feast and make happy, the gypsies celebrate. Especially at the birth of a child of a future *bulibasha*.

The old women try to stop Nicu from entering the room where Nadja and the baby lie, a place that is unclean and where gypsy men do not go. They block the doorway with their numbers, the sheer volume of their fat gypsy bodies. They *tut-tut* to divert him, but he is the son of the *bulibasha*, and the future leader himself. He can't be kept out of a room if he doesn't want to be kept out of a room. He must be obeyed. So they let him pass.

Nicu feels a jolt when he sees Nadja, how pale she is, how thin her face, how small her body, the baby out of her belly. He thinks to reach for her but doesn't, for he is gypsy, and believes as the gypsies believe. She is unclean, not to be touched, not yet, not even in an embrace or a kiss.

Nadja lifts the blanket from the baby's pale face. She watches Nicu, sees it in his eyes, the questions. But he loves her too, and that's the crux, and it always is, the double-edge sword, the pull in two directions.

Nadja is a gypsy. She knows well enough a traveller can't travel in two directions. The traveller must choose - one way or the other. And if there is a choice between a road and a meadow, staying and leaving, the gypsy takes the road. And if she comes to a fork, the gypsy never regrets the road taken, never looks back and wishes she had gone in the other direction, north instead of south, east instead of west.

Nicu's grandmother emerges from the walls.

"There is a way," she tells Nicu. "Give me the baby and I will sell her to the baby-dealer. It will be as if the child was never born, and you'll never hear another word about it from the gypsies. You are young and can have many more children, gypsy children, as dark as you, as beautiful as Nadja."

Nicu is thinking like a future *bulibasha*. He's choosing his direction. And Nadja is choosing hers.

Chapter 40

Nadja slips out into the night, her baby wrapped tightly in a gypsy's shawl to protect it from evil. She marvels that the baby squirms so strongly in her arms, but what should she expect? This is Nadja's child, Nicu's child, a gypsy child, and there is a journey ahead, a road to travel. Not even a curse can take the gypsy out of the child.

It's simple for Nadja to leave the back room of Nicu's family's house, for no one expects her to travel from her bed, let alone out the door, and out of their lives, and into another story. She stays in the shadows, close to the bushes. Travels through the courtyard, slips around the edges of the abandoned trailers, the abandoned cars, like shadow herself.

Nadja stops at one car in particular, lies the baby on the ground against the flat wheel. She slips her fingers under the hood and lifts, stops at the scratch of the hinges against the silence. But if the gypsies hear, they only roll over in their beds, curse the cats and their screeching lovemaking.

Nadja feels under the hood. Removes the money, hides the roll under her skirts where no gypsy man will look for it since Nadja has just given birth. She straps a knife to her leg for any *gadjo* who dares to go there.

Nadja keeps herself covered, shawl pulled over her head like a Muslim traveller, hiding her face, baby hidden in the folds of her clothes. She winds her way through the back paths and back alleys, circles to the caravan at the edge of the village, sets out with the travelling gypsies at the greying of the sky.

*****

The young wives don't notice that Nadja is gone until late morning. The room is quiet, and they think mother and child sleep. Or maybe the baby is dead, and they'll wait for Nadja to wake to discover it for herself.

The young wives busy themselves with chores, and make low whispers about the baby-dealer. They kiss their children, watch them more closely, scold them if they run too far, threaten to sell them if they're bad. The older children shiver, because they have heard the whispers about the baby-dealer, tell the stories to each other in the dark.

It's almost noon, and the young wives grow impatient with Nadja and her sleeping, enter the darkened room, curtains pulled shut, light shut out. They say her name, for she is a young wife, too, and should be awake. Weren't they out of bed the very next day when they spit out their babies?

But Nadja doesn't answer, and now they think her impudent. How dare she, she who slept with the *gadjo*? And gave birth to a child the colour of the moon, the colour of straw, the colour of cheese, tufts of hair the colour of cornsilk.

They fling open the curtains, let in the sun, chase away the shadows. But the bed is empty. They stir the blankets, push them down with the flat of their palms, as if Nadja and baby might just be hiding.

Nicu's grandmother sweeps into the room at the commotion. She has left the shadows of Nadja's dreams for only a few hours, and now Nadja's gone, and the baby, too. She curses. Flings the window open. Sends out her curse, and it flies away, looking for gypsy mother and her pale daughter. But the caravan has travelled far by now, and the curse can't find them. It lands instead upon the head of a baby-dealer, who has travelled through the night to meet an old gypsy woman. The haggling is done and the bargain struck for a fair-haired child, an aberration born to a young gypsy couple, and like most aberrations, worth her weight in gold. He plans to auction her among the rich desperate American housewives who can't have babies of their own.

No one notices the hood left wide open and yawning among the abandoned cars, except Nicu, who gently closes it, hinges screeching. He sits on the ground next to the flat wheel, leans against the rusted car door. Thinks about Nadja, and their pale baby. Thinks about following their trail, the gypsy *patrin*, joining them in whatever journey.

But he doesn't, for in the end, he is the *bulibasha's* son, and the future *bulibasha*, and his place is with his gypsies.

Nadja doesn't stay long with a single caravan. She moves from gypsy clan to gypsy clan. Crisscrosses her way across countries, over borders and back again, and doesn't even realize it, for the black lines of the map, the clearly marked perimeters that define people and their spaces, don't really exist.

Along her travels, on gusts of wind, Nadja hears stories about the beautiful wife of a future *bulibasha*. How exquisitely she danced, how she made the gypsies weep because they felt the open road, and all it was to be gypsy. How the dark ate her, and her baby. And once, she even heard it said that the moon is the face of a pale gypsy child swallowed by the night.

PART THREE

The End of Story

Chapter 41

You unearth the plastic baggie filled with dried leaves and stalks from beneath the couch cushions. We laugh at the silliness of the hiding place, and then roll a joint. You lick the paper, seal the edge, twist the ends. Your hands are big, but you do it quickly. I know those hands, their deftness. A red tulip sits in a glass on the turned-over milk crate. I picked the tulip from the city garden in the park, the picking an act of domesticity from the undomesticated. You light the joint, breathe deeply, and then hand it to me. I pinch the roach clip, draw in smoke, hold it in my lungs. I finally exhale, and we laugh, and open the windows. The breeze flutters the curtains.

It was a fine apple, you say. We both hoot, because it was bruised and lopsided, and your words are a lie. *And a fine story too,* you add.

"But the story's not done," I answer. "Figure it out if you can. Pick the truth from the untruth like crows picking clean the bones of a lesser bird. Swallow the story and leave only the lie, sun-bleached and bone-dry."

And I tell you more.

Chapter 42

Nadja met the pale man on a boat on the Danube River, the place where the Danube flows through the edges of Hungary, washes into Slovakia. River on its way to Budapest, where they have both already been, but not together. It is possible that they passed by each other on the street, stood in the same ticket queue, even touched without knowing. But they have yet to meet, to learn names, only now climb the small flight of stairs to the upper deck, both preferring to feel the air on their face than to sit behind glass in the crowded boat's belly below.

In these days, Nadja's days, Slovakia doesn't exist, except in the murmurs of dissatisfaction of nationalists. It is the time in story before the walls fall, and people rebel, before a tidal wave tears countrywomen apart, and their countries, too.

Nadja and the man that she is yet to meet float into Czechoslovakia, a place that now exists only in the imagination, for borders change, and maps, too. They will meet soon enough along this very stretch of river in this imaginary land.

They travel against the current, the Danube travelling in the opposite direction, searching the Black Sea, wanting the sea like all rivers do. They take the boat into Austria, stop awhile in Vienna, and then continue on their way. Sail into Germany, careful not to get tangled in the map's border like fish tangled in fishnet. Pass further along the Danube, not far from the remains of concentration camps, ovens where the Rom were burned alongside the Jews.

Did you know that?

Rom burnt in ovens, but not before they were studied and catalogued first. Blood samples stolen, and bone structure, too, plaster masks spread across their face to capture their bones, the flow of their skeleton. Gypsies meticulously studied to figure out why they travel. Won't take root, like Nana's plant cuttings, stems bleeding, raw and open, put into stale water on the windowsill to sprout, roots thick and dense like a jungle, crowding against the sides of the glass. Why the Rom live in makeshift homes, if homes at all, work at makeshift jobs, nothing stable and enduring, portable trades you can carry on your back, take with you, pull out of your knapsack and chuck if you wish. Apple picking, and basket weaving, and bricklaying, and brush making, and fortune telling, and horse dealing, and metal working, and jewellery making, and music making, and juggling, and selling, and storytelling, and scamming. What it is that is inside the gypsy to make her act this way, *be* this way. If it can be quantified, an enzyme in the blood, a flaw in the gene sequence, an abnormality. If it can be isolated, sliced open, removed from the body like the heart, or the bladder, or the liver, or the brain, stripped out like veins and arteries, put under the microscope and examined.

Nazis recorded the vast and wandering gypsy lineage in their ledgers, made neat careful entries. They did this so they wouldn't contact Rom blood, so they could identify who was gypsy, and who was not, as if Rom can be known by a name entered in a ledger.

Chapter 43

The boat upon which Nadja and the pale man met was small because the Danube is small, nothing like the ocean, where they would later sail in a giant liner, their passage paid by Nana and Pear, happy to hear from their prodigal son after all these years, and to have a grandchild, too. And a daughter-in-law to boot.

Right now, Nadja's glance lingers on the bread and cheese that the pale man takes from his backpack, puts on a cloth napkin spread across the top of his legs. Balances the food there, like some kind of juggler's trick, and I think of Mildred, and how she balanced her funeral feast, and it must be in the genes.

The backpack sits against his feet. The flap is open, the drawstring loose. Nadja sees the wallet, lazily open too, atop a sweater. She reads the name on the birth certificate, tucks it into her mind, Michael.

The backpack is the same as all Americans carry, large and held firm with an aluminum frame. It's a well-known fact among the Rom that Americans are rich, have lots of money to scam, even the ones who carry backpacks, and wear faded jeans, and travel cheaply. A red maple leaf is sewn to the backpack, and Nadja realizes with the swoop of disappointment that the pale man is Canadian. But they are almost the same, Canadian and American. The Americans are easier to flatter, although the Canadians will believe anything you tell them, wouldn't recognize a liar if she sat down beside him on a boat on the Danube.

The man thinks to offer bread and cheese to the woman sitting there beside him on a boat floating down the Danube – a woman young enough to be the baby's sister and not her mother, and pretty enough too. He breaks off a chunk from the long skinny loaf, and hands the woman the slab of cheese.

Nadja pulls her gypsy skirts up past her gypsy knees. She slips her gypsy knife out of the strap at the side of her gypsy legs, slices some cheese, and eats.

I think it was the knife that sealed fate, for a woman with a knife is hard to resist and has her own charm. She knows her mind, knows her knife, will act upon them. She travels alone, for otherwise, why would she need a knife? A knife demonstrates independence, and independence is attractive to a man with a backpack travelling a foreign land. Until he gets home, where everything is different, and always the same. Where independence is harder to withstand, even in a woman, and especially in a wife.

The baby cries, hungry to remind the world of her presence, remind us of story. Nadja lifts her off the bench, slips her under her shirt, and the crying stops. Nadja's breast, Nadja's milk – Nadja - is all the world, all the story, that the baby needs.

"What's its name," the pale man asks.

"Her," Nadja says. "She's a girl, and her name is Michaela."

It's a pretty name, as pretty as any other, I've always thought. The pale man thinks so, too. He laughs at the coincidence, for he is not Rom, and thinks that a coincidence is just that.

"My name is Michael," he says.

And so the three of us are bound together by a scam as simple as a name.

*****

The early events of my life account for my love of the sea. Why I have always wanted to travel to the ocean, even when I was a little girl, *especially* when I was a little girl, perched on a windowsill, like a secret, face as pale as the moon. Breathed in the ocean air, even though I lived dead center in a large country as far away from ocean as I could possibly be. But I knew the winds travelled far and high, that the birds caught these winds, rode the currents to oceans, across oceans, never once touching twig-feet to ground, then rode the currents back again. So it made every sense to me that I could smell the ocean lifted upon the wind, even here, to this unlikely place, if I only put my nose out the window, put my face to the sky, and breathed in deeply.

It was a long journey across the Atlantic, but the sea rocked me in my mother's arms, as constant as the rocking chair. Sometimes the seas were rough, battered the ocean liner, with its many levels, with its long narrow hull, our berth in the deepest part, furthest from the upper decks, for the bowels were the place of the lesser fares. Have you seen an ocean liner? How tall and magnificent it is? How sleek and royal? *Bulibasha*, if it were gypsy. Not at all like the fat squat lakers that travel the Great Lakes, through the network of canals and locks, as far as the St. Lawrence, unloading their cargo at ports along the way, their grain or logs, but never to travel across a sea.

The waves slapped against the ship and sometimes sloshed over the decks, getting us wet with salt water, and we'd lick our lips, and taste it, and my mother would lick my cheek to taste it from my skin.

Sometimes the ocean was as clear as glass, as smooth as polished stone, and the stars would twinkle in the black sky, like so many candles. I can understand, having seen the velvet sky and twinkling stars spread above me from the view of my mother's arms, how sailors could read the stars as map. Chart their course, know true North, find their way.

The sea captain married them, right beside the captain's

polished brass navigator's wheel, and no one thought to ask if Nadja was already married. And she never thought to say a word about Nicu, and if she did think to say, she thought against it.

When the wayward son and his young family landed, they took a train-week's journey across rock and through firs. They chugged through Pear's province where the people speak French, and then chugged through Nana's province where the people speak English.

They finally disembarked at a one-room train station in the very middle of a very big country, their bodies cramped, and their legs needing to stretch.

Nana took the baby in her arms, pulled back the layers of gypsy shawl. Looked long at the little moon face, fat-cheeked with Nadja's milk. Looked long at the yellow tufts of hair sticking from baby head like corn silk.

Looked long at Nadja's dark gypsy skin. Looked long at her son, skin the colour of barn straw, the colour of cheese, the colour of the moon, his hair like corn silk.

"What's her name?" Nana asked.

"Michaela," Nana's son says, his own name Michael.

And nothing more was ever said about the who or what of me.

Chapter 44

"How did your mother die again?"

Thomas asks a lot of questions lately. I wonder his intention. Thomas is a man of intention. There's always a reason behind his words, and if not *a* reason, then reasoning. It's part of scholarship. Part of his training and his inclination.

"Heart attack."

"That's odd," he says. "For such a young woman."

"Yes," I tell him. It is odd.

Thomas waits for more, so I give him more.

"She was young, very young, seventeen, maybe eighteen, no older. Gave birth to me when she was fourteen. Could have had an abortion, I suppose, some kitchen table operation performed by an old gypsy grandmother, but she didn't."

"Nadja. With a hard 'j'," he pauses to ponder. "What kind of name is that?"

"Romanian. My mother grew up in a small village in Romania. In fact, that's where I was born, too, but I came to Canada as a baby at her breast."

Thomas tilts his head, looks at me quizzically, then is uncharacteristically quiet.

*****

When I try to isolate moments, the point in the journey where the seducer becomes the seduced, then it was *that* moment, the moment of the gift of a book. I didn't expect to fall in love with Thomas. It crept up on me, and then it was there, if what we had is love. I don't know.

Thomas simply handed the book to me. For once, there were no fluorescent notes flapping from the pages. He thought I was ready, trusted me to find my own way. I felt I had arrived. This, from the girl who's always leaving.

He must have searched long and hard to find that particular book. It's not a title you'd unearth at the corner store among the Harlequins. He had to plan the gift, and then commit to it. Implement it carefully so the giving was a surprise. Telephone the bookstores, locate the one that would order such an obscure title, place a special order. Check daily to see if the book arrived so the store doesn't phone and tip me off. I understand it now, Thomas's commitment. It's much the same as my commitment to the journey, and they're both a way of life.

Such a simple gesture, no fanfare, a thin book enclosed in a brown paper bag, handed over the fold-up kitchen card table where we ate our meals. There was nothing seemingly momentous in the act itself. I suppose it's always the simple act – as simple as a book passed between two hands – that you later look back upon and recognize for what it is, the momentous couched in the ordinary. One of those things that you don't normally see, but is there all along, something alive and magical. The ability of a dime to flutter through the air, more feather than coin. The impossible held within the possible, the Kingdom of God within the mustard seed. It's a common message among Gnostic literature such as *The Gospel of Thomas*. Heaven is not a location, a place of roots and soil, a house with stonewalls and a garden around it. Heaven is transportable. You carry it with you. And Jesus is a gypsy!

It's ironic, I suppose, that *The Gospel of Thomas* is the

very book that he gave me. A parting gift perhaps, although the parting is not yet acknowledged, certainly not by Thomas, who doesn't know such things as partings. He views leavings as failures instead of part and parcel of the journey, the Traveller's way.

Chapter 45

Thomas thinks I am ready for the Gnostics, having been first carefully introduced to the history and the politics of Judea at the time of the historical Jesus. The religious factions, the Roman occupation, the Pharisees, the Sadducees, the Essenes, then the traditional gospel writers, Matthew, Mark, and Luke, and next John, and the letters of Paul.

He thinks he's provided me with a reliable foundation of orthodoxy. I'm now suitably anchored, ready to withstand heresy. He doesn't understand that I'm the heretic. It's my nature. I cannot be anchored.

I follow the trail of breadcrumbs that Thomas lays out for me, goes where he leads. He takes me by the hand. It's a different kind of journey and we wind along the road of thought and mind. He introduces me to religious philosophies in the same methodical way in which he lives, books and ideas laid out for me like stepping-stones. Perhaps more like the socks in his dresser, neatly rolled together and matched, never any holes.

"*The Gospel of Thomas* belongs to the Gnostic camp," Thomas says.

It becomes increasingly clear to me as I read the books

that Thomas has given me, that the choice of word is exactly right: Camp. The fight for orthodoxy was a battle, and the Gnostics lost. And so the story changes. What we know as truth, is simply the truth that won, and no greater truth than that.

"The battle raged in the first few centuries after the crucifixion," Thomas says. "Beliefs were carved, and theologies formed. Pivotal doctrines adopted, often simply by vote of a church council. The Virgin Birth and Immaculate Conception cost Saint Augustine a hundred thoroughbred Arabian horses, but he won the vote. Until then, Mary was a woman like any other, and look at her now."

He sits on the floor, glass of wine in hand. His eyes flare with the excitement of the battle, but not a battle that is the thrust of sword through skin, sword pulled out again, blood pumping from wound, red and sticky. Body is not the terrain of Thomas.

I see the flush of his face, the flare of his eyes, his animation, the punctuation of the air with his hand. Fingers like knife, slicing into idea.

Thomas is excited by arguments. Feels the rush of adrenaline. Mistakes body for mind, and the passion of interaction as desire. So did I, in the midst of it, caught up in his excitement.

"Early Christians didn't immediately believe in the resurrection of the physical body," Thomas says. "It's a big jump from an empty tomb to a flesh-and-blood risen Christ."

"Urban legend," I say.

Thomas stops his commentary. I know I have him then, when he stops his explanation, when I stop him dead in his tracks. He grins, a rogue smile that sweeps across his face with sudden delight. It's this sudden delight that delights me, that seduces me like dance. I come to wait for that grin, to watch his face for signs of it, the Second Coming of smile, to try to pull it out of him, to bring it on like the apocalypse. It's our foreplay, and I read Thomas's books with an eye towards it, listen to our conversations in the same way. Look for the bit of information that will delight him, stop him in his tracks. Look for the winding of thought that is new trail to him. That sudden something that sets the heart pounding, the body soaring, like an unexpected kiss. That's the way it was with Thomas and me. Ideas and conversation like an unexpected kiss.

"Think about it," I tell Thomas, and Thomas thinks about it, I can tell by his eyes, intensity focused on my face.

He waits for my words, hangs on to them, words not like poetry, but the passion of reasoned argument. So I give him my words, my explanations. "An empty tomb, a supposed Jesus sighting. And so the tale grows, takes on a life of its own. Takes on flesh and blood, until the story is a living breathing being."

Thomas is quiet, simply listens. So I continue. "Each new telling like dipping fingers afresh into the open wounds and saying *yes*, this is truth."

"*Yes*," Thomas says.

He nods his head, settling into the thought of it.

*****

It is all very interesting, Gnosticism. Our conversations empty many bottles of wine, outlast many candles and many nights.

Thomas tells me that the Gnostics were the dominant force during the first centuries of Christianity. Gnosticism reached its peak at 200 CE, but fortunes turn, and two hundred years later, orthodox Christianity is declared the religion of the Roman Empire. The Gnostics are now heretics, their truths heretical, and their believers fed to the lions.

Until Nag Hammadi, all that scholars knew about the Gnostic movement was extrapolated by reading between the lines of the writings of the early Church fathers. Story extracted by turning over the stones of diatribe, looking beneath the words of condemnation for the Gnostic earth beneath.

In 1945, by happenstance, an earthenware jar is found near the shores of the Nile, a river searching out the Mediterranean Sea. The discovery is made where the river bends towards a small village. The discoverer is an impoverished man looking for fertilizer, and not large reddish jars. But he takes what he is given, digs it up anyway. Pulls the jar out of the earth. Sets it down on solid ground, jar top tightly shut and sealed, ponders what he has unearthed.

Muhammed Ali, for that is his true name, thinks to shatter the jar, to scatter the pot and reveal its secrets. But he's afraid, for maybe an evil curse is confined within its walls, will flutter out like bat and land on his head, and that is the secret of the earthenware jar. But the lure of gold and treasure shore up his bravery, and he strikes the jar in spite of curse, hits it with his hatchet. Flakes of golden parchment flutter in the open air, twist and turn as if they breathe.

The Egyptian is disappointed. Books. Scrolls and manuscripts bound in leather. He flips some open, can't read the script, can't read any script at all, for he can't read. But the books look ancient, and he gathers them up, hopes he can turn a profit, execute the scam. Muhammed Ali unrolls the turban from his head, lays it on ground, scoops up the pieces of broken shard and book, wraps them in the turban like a hobo's pack, slings the pack over his shoulder.

In his village, called Nag Hammadi, he shows the contents of turban to his mother. "We can't eat these," the old woman says, spitting out her words along with her spittle. "And they won't keep us warm."

She turns her back to her useless son and these useless books. Fertilizer is lucrative, she thinks, and curses the day she gave birth. But she is resourceful, too, for how do you think she survived a lifetime in the deserts?

She smiles toothlessly, a charming scammer's smile, bends to touch the useless treasure, to figure out a use. Holds one of the leather volumes in her leather hands, turns it over, unties the leather string. Looks at the curious scribbling, the even rows of ancient script laid across the page like stonework. Her bones are cold, and maybe the scraps of papyrus can keep her warm after all, if not fill her stomach. Rips a chunk of parchment from the leather binding, tosses it into the fire.

*****

The remaining pieces of the Nag Hammadi library, as they come to be known, are bartered and sold in bits and dribbles, an ancient codex here, a hitherto unknown Christian gospel there.

Over the decades, the manuscripts are gathered together again, except for the chunks burned as fuel to warm an old woman in the night desert of Egypt.

Scholars pour over the texts, like scholars do. Translate the archaic Coptic writing into modern language, ecstatic over the discovery of these wisdom texts. But although worthy of the wine and an interesting tale, it's not *this* story, the discovery of the Gnostic writings, that takes my breath away, that leaves me breathless. They are not the words that whisper in my ear like revelation. The words that send my heart crashing, my body swooping, adrenaline pumping, little girl in wheelbarrow, drunk with blue sky and white cloud, dizzy with the speed, *faster, faster, Pear.*

I read *The Gospel of Thomas*, stare at the part of story that has this effect upon me, that makes my heart swoop like an unexpected kiss.

The words whisper in my ear as if I'm the favoured disciple. Gypsy words. Hidden in an earthenware jar in an Egyptian desert for more than a thousand years.

And this is what they say:

Become passersby.

Chapter 46

We are drunk with ideas when Thomas and I finally make love. He leans towards me, and I think he has lost his balance. We don't even make it into the bed. Do it right there, on the floor, in the space between the coffee table and the sofa. Fumble through it. It's over before it begins. Thomas is a virgin. It's easy to tell. So much for seduction. I've slept in his bed for two full months, naked next to him, blankets entangled around both of us, skin touching, arms and legs flopping over each other, and no reaction. And here I am, wearing androgynous clothes - sweatpants, Thomas's flannel shirt, and thick wool work socks, the kind factory workers wear, men who cut down trees, dig ditches, do other masculine things. We're heatedly discussing the gnostics and their desire for androgyny, and he unexpectedly acts in this non-androgynous way.

But Thomas gets better. Like the dedicated student he is, he returns to his lessons often, every night in fact. He studies hard. I show him how to make love, guide his hands. Now he's the pupil and I'm the teacher. Body is my terrain.

There's a sweetness about his lovemaking, an awkwardness that never leaves. A vulnerability, and then an earnestness, his willingness to learn. How he finally loses himself, whispers my name over and over again, my name as he knows it, *Mary.*

And sometimes when he slips into dreaming, he calls for me again, his voice at the edge of panic, as if I'm lost to him. I brush my fingers against his skin, follow his spine, tell him not to worry. I am here.

Chapter 47

I run from Nana and her precious photo of the pale blonde man, more precious than me, more precious than my mother. Escape Nana's mirror, her lies, escape her house (never my house), the screen door flapping madly behind me. Race as far away as I can get from them all, through the orchard and over the stone fence, through the woods, into a long cornfield, tumble out into a farmer's field. Race across the vast expanse of field into an old grey barn, collapse into a stack of hay, sink deep, finally stop running. The sun is soft and slips through the wood in the places where the roof is caving in, the barn long abandoned, and my breathing slows down, my heart rate settles. Exhausted, I let the sun fade away, slip into sleep, a place where there are no silver-framed photos, no dead mothers or receding fathers, no children left behind.

*****

I awake in the early dawn to a dog licking my face. He stands on my chest, peers into my eyes, as if looking to see if anyone is in there. I sit up and the dog jumps off me, jumps around happily, hay clinging to his fur. He camouflages well with the straw, although I suspect him to be a lighter shade if he were clean, the sun-dried sand of an ocean beach. I've never had a dog before, and fall easily into the having. Dog falls easily into the having, too. We're in this together, both abandoned.

My stomach growls.

With no mother and father to bring us breakfast, Dog and I are left to our own devices. Feast or famine is the way of the gypsy, and right now it is famine, so we set out to search for feast. Dog sticks close to me, as if I might disappear as suddenly as I came to him, pop in and out of story. We go out into the morning world, trudge up a hill and trot down the other side to a path that leads through a field of white daisies, and then to a gravel road. A stone slips into my shoe and I shake it out. Hop on one foot, do a crazy rain dance. Dog thinks I play, and so I do, hop in circles for him. He jumps up, dances with me, his front paws on my chest, leaving dirt marks.

Our breakfast arrives unexpectedly on the horizon, but that is how it happens on the road, when you least expect it. I think at first it is my imagination, an apparition, but Dog growls, and then barks excitedly. He sees them too, the girls on their way to school, packed lunches in their bulging knapsacks.

Dog and I hide beneath the bushes, press our bodies flat to the ground. The dirt feels damp, smells rich and earthy like worms have tilled it. Dog is taut beside me, and I know he wants to spring. I put my hand against his neck, and it calms him, and he waits for my signal. He is happy, here with me, waiting for my go-ahead, happy to be part of a pack. The end of his tail flicks against my bare legs.

The girls draw closer to us and I can hear their chatter, make out their words, skipping songs and birthday parties and other nonsense. I cannot believe they don't notice Dog and me, peering out from under the bushes, but I suppose you don't see what you don't suspect. They are three-two-one step away, and then they are even with us. Now they pass by and it is the perfect moment to attack. They won't even know what hit them.

Dog whimpers.

The girl with hair the color of a raven turns in our

direction, and our eyes meet. She looks surprised, but not afraid. I leap from the bush, Dog leaping with me. For some reason, I don't grab her knapsack, grab her companion's instead, rip it fiercely from her back.

The little coward screams and runs away, abandons her friend to suffer the consequences of Dog and me. "Give me your knapsack or my killer dog will kill you," I snarl.

"No, he won't," the raven-haired girl says.

"He's a trained assassin."

She only smiles.

"Bite!" I order.

Dog jumps at the girl. Licks her face. She pets him under the chin, then continues on her way, her hair long and flowing down her back, her knapsack intact. Dog thinks about going with her. Trots a few steps, then returns. I forgive him his disloyalty, rifle through our victor's spoils. Scatter the contents of the coward's knapsack, the thick red pencils, crayons, homework papers, hair ribbons, barrettes. Keep only the paper bag lunch.

Dog and I return to the old barn. There, we eat. And when we are done, our thirst quenched, and our hunger gone, we lie back in the hay and I tell Dog gypsy stories.

That's the way we live – ambush when our stomach tells us. Eat, tell stories, sleep, do it again. It's a good life, a dog's life, and I grow more content with every story told, and every knapsack stolen.

*****

"Run for your life!"

I stir a bit from my sleep. Lift my head off the straw to look at Dog. He perks his ears to attention, but nothing more. Doesn't yap, jump madly, herd me out of the barn to see what or who intrudes upon this little country we've drawn for ourselves, these lovely borders. He doesn't want this to end, all loose ends tucked and put away into story.

"Head for the hills!"

I think I must be dreaming. In the midst of dream, it

occurs to me there are no hills, just a cornfield and a cow-field and a daisy meadow and a road where we lie in wait to raid for lunches. We've lived here for a week now, Dog and me, although I suspect it's time for us to move along, to pack up our borders, take a trip down the road, find another barn in another country. Word has spread of the pirates along the gravel road, although I correct the mistake, shout "*Gypsies!*" as I chase the *gadjo* brats and steal their lunches. Wield stick like knife in my fist, sheath the stick in my sock beside my calf when I've done. We're the bogeyman, the baby dealer, the old gypsy waiting in the shadows, all the horrible fears of all the children rolled up into Dog and girl. We have only to jump from ditch and the cowards yield their knapsacks, feel lucky to escape with their lives.

"Run! They know about you. They're coming."

The girl with the raven-hair stands over me in the hay. Grabs my shoulders, shakes me from sleep. Dog jumps up and licks her face. Through the wooden slats, I see a police car. The door opens and Nana and Pear step out. A policeman, too. I think he has a gun, surely he has a gun. They've come to make me go back.

"Will you take Dog?" I ask the girl. "Help him escape?"

She nods, and I tell Dog to go with her, *now, fast, hurry, run.* Dog lingers, torn between going and staying. But he's a gypsy dog, and knows that when the choice is going or leaving, and the scales are evenly tipped, then the choice is clear.

"What's your name?" I ask.

"Lily," she calls back.

And then Dog and Lily are gone.

Chapter 48

When I am a few years older, I run further away, past the pear tree, past the *Michaela*, around the circular gravel road in front of the manor where Pear pushed me in the wheelbarrow, *faster, faster, faster*, through the stone gates. Then I stop to calm the surge of adrenaline at the adventure of my escape, and I look to the night sky, locate Polaris. Situate myself. Head out north, let the star lead me.

The road is empty, and I'm quick to dive into the ditch if a car or truck comes in my direction. Sometimes, I take the shortcut through the woods. Then, the trees block the stars from view. My flashlight lights the pathway a few steps ahead of me, but that's all. For the most part, the night is pitch black. The blackness frightens me, but love for Dog, and then love for Dog and Lily, move me through journey. In time, I learn to travel with fear as my companion, welcome its breath against the hollow of my cheek. Come to know that fear is like your footsteps, your own breathing. You can't escape it. You need to feed upon its energy.

I travel to the church on the outskirts of town. Inside, I tiptoe by the font where they drown babies, past the alms box where church people steal money from the poor and keep it for themselves. Count up eleven pews from the back row, turn left from the center aisle and lie low, wait.

This night, the Reverend glides by. He's a fat man that eats children as easily as he eats communion wafers. He doesn't see me, pressed flat against the pew. I'm a piece of paper, just the varnish on the pew, just the pew itself. Such is my resolve, my commitment to Dog and Lily. I'll defend them to my death if the Reverend catches them, but he pushes through the door before they arrive, a wind rushing in to fill the vacuum left by the air he displaces.

Lily, such a silly name, a flower's name, but it's the right name for Lily. Her skin is porcelain white, as white as the flower's petals, and her hair is jet black, the kind of hair I have always coveted, want for my own, even now, even today. Hair that isn't the colour of the moon, the colour of straw, the colour of cheese, the colour of corn silk. Gypsy hair.

The contrast against Lily's skin makes the black even blacker. Her hair shines black, glistens black, like the feathers of a raven, or the luster on coal.

Lily opens the door a crack. Dog can't wait, bounds through the space between door and church, and we play our game. He sniffs for me, sniffs the air, sniffs the hardwood floor, sniffs his way through the rows of pews.

He pretends well, plays the part of the hunter dog. Prolongs the game, savours it. Dog knows exactly where I am. He leaps over the last pew, unable to contain his dog excitement, his dog adrenaline any longer, licks my face and whines and jumps. He pushes his nose into my pocket, and I give him a treat.

Lily sits beside me, and her hair is long and messy. It touches my shoulder. I pretend it is my hair, black against my moon skin. We've been running away together for almost two years now, whenever Lily can get away, meeting like this in the dead of night.

Sometimes we pretend we're clergy. Light the candles, our noses in the air like the holy fathers. The flames cast eerie shadows, but instead of being scared, the dancing shadows comfort us. And once in a while, when it is time to leave, we forget to blow out the candles, and they're still burning in the morning, and it's another one of Mildred's miracles, a sign from God, candles that light without human hand.

Chapter 49

"Did you see your mother today?" Lily asks me, the two of us stretched out on our backs in front of the altar, Dog curled beside us.

"Yep," I tell her. "At the grocers. She was picking out the reddest juiciest apples, just the way I like them. She looked at each one to make sure it was perfect before she put it in her basket, and she wore a sweater as red as the apples, and her lips were red, too, and her hair jet black, just like your hair."

Sometimes the woman is a figment of my imagination, and I make her up for Lily. Other times, I watch for the perfect woman throughout the day, choose her from all the people who pass me by. The woman who would be most like my mother, if she were alive – and then I tell Lily.

And Dog, too, who always listens.

One night, many night journeys later, I wait in the pews longer than usual, pressed flat against the pew, and I fall asleep. I awake with a start, and there is Lily, sitting beside me. She's alone. I sit up and look toward the door.

"Where's Dog?" I ask.

Then I look at Lily again. Her face is wet.

I put my arm around her, and she cries openly, loud

sobs into my shoulder. Her body moves like waves.

I stroke her black hair with my palm, and at the bottom of each stroke, feel her neck, small and fragile in my hands. My shirt is wet with her tears, and I comfort her the best I can, since I knew grief first, and now she does, too.

Lily can't stop crying. I lift her face from my shoulder, cup her small chin in my small hands. My fingers brush her cheekbones. I brush her tears not to rid her of them, but to rub them *into* her. Rub them into my skin, too, through my fingertips.

It's something we share, her tears, this grief. They're part of our bodies. Can't be separated from us without maiming who we are, dishonouring where we've been, where we've travelled.

Dog is dead, but we take him with us on the road, in the same way we take each other. Salt and tears absorbed through our skin, the rush of adrenaline and love.

Then I do something that has no explanation, no reason, for love is not reasonable, and neither is the expression of it. I kiss Lily, full on the lips, like lovers do in the movies. It's the only model I have for love, the only action I have for responding to what I feel, this surge of emotion.

Lily's lips are salty with her grief, and now I know the taste of grief, too, and it tastes like the ocean. It doesn't surprise me that Lily's lips would taste like the ocean, nor that love and grief would taste the same.

Chapter 50

It takes several nights of lovemaking for me to realize what's happening. Ideas make Thomas real. They are aphrodisiac to him. He thinks that I'm the aphrodisiac, but I'm just the spokeswoman. Tonight the topic of desire is figs.

We do our slow dance. Wait until evening, and then light the candles, turn off the lamp. Thomas opens a bottle of wine, and lets it breathe, or so he says, although it's really an act of anticipation. When the wine has breathed enough, breathed in the air, breathed in our anticipation, then Thomas fills the glasses. We sip wine between words, words that are slow at first. And so it begins.

"If I should wish a fruit brought to paradise it would certainly be the fig," Thomas says, paraphrasing the prophet Muhammad.

"The fig only masquerades as fruit," I tell Thomas. I, too, have done my homework. "The fig is actually a flower that is inverted into itself."

Truth and lies once again, flower masquerading as fruit.

"Some say the bodhi tree which sheltered Buddha and under which he found enlightenment is a type of fig tree," I add.

We move along to Cleopatra, the seductress seduced by her favorite fruit. How she died for the fruit, died by it, the asp carried to her in a basket of figs. Imagine, asp wrapped around the inside of the basket, body curving to bowl shape, head like fig. Cleopatra reaching. Forbidden fruit lifting its head, pausing just before it strikes.

We talk about Eve, the original seductress and the original seduction. Discuss the act of her picking forbidden fruit from the tree.

"Artists have it all wrong," Thomas says. "First, there's the apple, hanging red-ripe from the tree. There's a theory it was really a fig."

Thomas pours wine and continues.

"Second, look at the common depiction of Eve. She's reaching for the fruit, serpent curled around the branch, tempting her with snake words. In reality, figs are often left to fall to the ground, and that's when they're harvested. Eve very well could have picked the fig off the ground to bite into it, not plucked it from a tree."

We talk more about figs.

At least a fat candle's worth.

How Adam and Eve sewed fig leaves together to make clothes when they realized they were naked and wanted to cover themselves. How the praises of figs were sung in a Babylonian hymnbook, one of the oldest samples of writing, even older than Genesis. How the ancient Greeks considered figs a gift of Demeter, and how figs were made sacred by Dionysus, the god of wine and good times. How figs were so valued that smuggling them out of the country was illegal, and how figs were awarded as prestigious prizes to the Olympic athletes. How the god Bacchus introduced figs to the Romans, and how Pliny wrote that eating figs will get rid of your wrinkles, and keep one young in looks and heart.

How the skin of a ripe fig is deep purple, and how the fruit hangs from the tree like an inverted heart. How the flesh is pinkish-white, and juicy, and sweet. How a wasp must crawl inside the fruit to pollinate the flower, and how only the female fruit is edible. How a fig ready for eating should be soft, but not too soft. How timing is everything. How you should smell the fruit, lift it to your nose, eat the fig before it ferments and while it's still fresh.

We know all this about figs, but not everything. We don't crawl inside the forbidden fruit, taste it from the inside, feel the texture in our mouths, the pulp sweet and soft against our tongues.

Chapter 51

"What's your name?"

I cannot lie, we're too much alike. It's in your flaming hair, your fierce eyes. It's in the way you wear the street so easily, no home other than your sleeping bag, no companion other than your black dog. It's in the way you disturb me, the way I search you out, again and again.

"Michaela," I say.

You swallow my name whole, take it into your body, absorb it into your cells, that's how immediately you know me. Then you pass me by, taking my name with you.

"And you?" I ask, too late.

I turn around to follow you with my stare. I think I see the flick of your dog's tail in the crowd, a flash of your red hair, but I imagine these things.

You're gone.

Like the seagull.

Chapter 52

You give me your jacket. It's a chivalry more suited to Thomas, with his quaint code of behavior, his outdated rules of engagement between men and women, engagement between a particular man and a particular woman. Between Thomas and his beloved.

It is a cold evening for June. The wind swirls debris about our feet, and an empty chip bag sails by, dust forming into small tornadoes in the corners of the buildings. Your black dog pads silently next to you. His face is square and his body box-like, and he's darker than the night. He accepts my presence because you accept it. He sniffs at the air to catch a whiff of what's ahead, tilts his head slightly, as if listening to something I'll never hear. He growls at some unseen danger, a low growl that is a warning on the edge of attack. You are his beloved, and he'll protect you.

I wonder what he knows with certainty, how he perceives the scents and sounds. Whether he translates them into images in his mind, so that he sees things before we see them, or in ways that we cannot.

Now that my scent is on you, in your clothes, in your skin, in your hair, I wonder if he smells my image. Sees me when he sniffs my sweater lying in yours, sleeves empty and wrapped around each other. Sees me through my scent on your blanket, the sleeping bag we wrap ourselves inside, trying to keep warm, our bodies like snakes. Sees my finer details. Knows where I'm going, and where I have been. Hears my intentions, his head cocked to one side. Sniffs the air for the truth and the untruth that lies about me in layers of perfume. Picks the strands apart, sniffs first one and then the other.

Something catches our eye in the dark. We watch it flip and swirl. The thing is fragile and delicate, small and white. We are mesmerized. It's as if it exerts power over us, and maybe it does, for how would we know? We've never seen such a thing. For all we know, it's the force that holds the world together. Keeps gravity in place and objects from being flung outward into distant space. Keeps the planets aligned, and the tides flowing, and the lines of longitude and latitude from collapsing into each other.

The thing swirls down the alleyway and through the dark. We walk quickly to keep pace. It's magic, the way it moves, and I know it's alive. There's no logic to its pattern, to the way it dances. It moves by its own laws, and not the ones that bind us. I think it's animal, and then bird or insect, and then ghost, and then spirit, like thought or soul or imagination filled out into form, but none fit exactly. I'm left with the magic. I don't doubt it. Not for an instant.

But then my eyes adjust, and the magic dispels. The wind batters about a piece of packing Styrofoam.

That's all.

I tell you about my mother, my father, the rocking chair, the dark. Things I haven't told any other, not even Thomas, especially not Thomas.

You take my hand. Your hand is big, and overwhelms mine. Your touch is easy. Your fingers are lean and strong, and I think you might play a fiddle, but you say no, you use your hands to twist copper wire into bits of art. It's your livelihood. Livelihood is not a common word among street people. "If you're an artist, make a livelihood at it, then why were you panhandling?" I ask.

Your laughter erupts unexpectedly. It matches your deep-red hair, the color of fire. "It's a kind of magic. I sit on the ground, put out an empty cup, and voila! People throw coins in it."

And then you laugh more. The air around us is electrified by the sound, as if electrons have shifted their charge, been disrupted. Lost ions, gained electrons, or whatever it is they do when a state is changed.

I think of the games that Pear played to amuse me when I was little, when he would rub a balloon on the collar of Nana's fur coat. *Voila*, he'd say, with a grand flourish, and the balloon would stick magically to my sweater. Then he'd run a comb against the fur, and make my hair stand up on end.

We walk out of the city center, and the geography shifts, like gradient of colour. The office buildings and chic cafes and derelict taverns and rundown rooming houses give way to strip malls and then renovated stone houses with historical plaques declaring heritage status, wraparound porches and overflowing flower boxes, steppingstone pathways and late model cars in the driveways. It's not unattractive, and I feel a twinge of longing for the same, but it's fleeting.

We walk further, and the geography shifts again. Historical houses turn into middle-income neighborhoods, low bungalows and high townhouses, and then newer subdivisions, where the garage is prominent, takes center stage. Evidence of children - bicycles and strollers - tumble across lawns. Then the children themselves, dinner finished, an hour to play before storybooks, and baths, and pajamas, and bed. Parents see us from their windows. Hurriedly call their children inside, safe from the bogeyman and bogeywoman. They think we're displaced, we are where we don't belong. We laugh again.

We walk out of all of this. Walk out of the day. Walk through it into the twilight and then into the dark, the shifting of time like the shifting of geography. Move through a greyscale of light and shadows into the night. Find magic. A piece of Styrofoam tumbling in the dark.

We reach a hill, a large hill, almost a mountain. Climb

it, the path winding around the hillside like a coil, slowly snaking towards the top. The path gives way to the hilltop and the lights of the city spread below us like distant candles. I recognize the patterns, the main roads and intersections, marked by the straight parade of the street lamps. The clusters of office buildings, square candles stacked on top of each other, and the mazes of houses, squat candles clumped together into their separate neighborhoods.

The lights are dazzling, but it is the night sky that steals my breath away. Steals me for itself, takes me as one of its own, an act of thievery. We turn our gaze away from the city lights, lie on our back, aware of our bodies against each other. Watch the stars and do not speak. You're a man of silence, as much as Thomas is a man of words. With us, there is no need to fill the night with candles or words.

The stars and the sky are enough.

Chapter 53

When I'm old enough to reach the doorknob, to turn the locks, I run away from the manor every night. I don't literally run, don't let the sound of my feet give away my intention. I keep adrenaline in check so that I glide silently past Nana and Pear's bedroom, a small pale ghost, barely visible in the shadows of the soft wall lamp. Never completely control the adrenaline. It is who I am - s*plit the wood, and it is there.*

Nana and Pear leave their bedroom door open so they can listen for me in their sleep, listen for my escape. Pear snores, a thick guttural French Canadian noise that helps to hide my footsteps. Nana breathes like the English, controlled and polite, small rushes of air that rise when Pear's snore subsides. They syncopate their sounds.

I leave their sounds behind, leave *them* behind, press quietly down the creaking stairs. I don't bolt, take care not to warn the sleeping enemy, tiptoe slowly, tiptoe lightly. It's hard not to run across the kitchen floor, to sprint the last few steps to the door. The room is thick with black, and it wraps itself around me, but I hold my fear in check, don't turn on the kitchen light, although the switch is within my reach. I know its location, have only to reach out. Feel the wall with the flat of my palm, flick on the switch to flood the kitchen with light, but I don't let myself. Finally reach the door, stretch for the knob, and it's glorious, the surge of adrenaline.

When I'm very young, I go no further than the courtyard. Sometimes I climb the pear tree, sit in the branches, and when the fruit is ripe, the pears hang around me like bells, glisten green in the moonlight. Other times I lie across the bow of the Michaela, stare up at the sky, stars spread above me like so many candle flames, and imagine I'm adrift on ocean. Imagine the rocking. Pull rocking deep from my memory.

At first, the stars have no pattern, no names, but then I draw the lines, connect the dots like the pages of the colouring books the Aunties give me. Draw the stars, find their shapes, and it's gentle, like caressing body with fingertips.

In the day, I seek out astronomy and astrology books. Study the books, read the names of the stars, look at the charts, memorize the names of the constellations. And every night, my head full of these names, I run away to the *Michaela,* and lie back, and rock, and name the sky. Sirius, Polaris, Vega. Bright stars to situate oneself by, to make map out of the night. They're my guideposts, my street lamps, and I look for them first. Then the lesser stars, and then the stars that are not stars, but masquerade as them. The planets, Jupiter and Venus, and my favourite, Mars, for its tinge of red.

I save the constellations for last. Savour them, like sucking chocolate, drawing out the taste. Pegasus, the Flying Horse. A celestial stone throw from the Circlet of Pisces, the Fishes, swimming in opposing directions, in opposition to each other, but when held together, viewed in the same frame, they're perfection. Leo, the Lion, roaring its stardust storms. And in honour of Dog - Canis Minor and Canis Major. Sirius, the Alpha star of the Alpha dog, not far from Orion. Mere million light years, so that if I were a star child, lived in the sky, I could leap the distance, stepping stones in a river. And then Eridanus, the sky River, winding through the night like the Danube through the European countryside, flowing into the lesser star Acamar, and then past Acamar to Achernar, the Black Sea, the brilliant star to which Eridanus is drawn.

Orion, the Hunter, trekking the sky in hunter pursuit. The red glow in the middle of Orion's sword, the Orion Nebula. Ursa Major, the Greater Bear, standing on his two hind legs, stretching upright, stretching large and powerful beneath the North Celestial Pole, the point around which all the stars circulate. It's a love that moves the skies. Ursa Minor, the Smaller Bear, and within the Bears, the Big Dipper and the Little Dipper, and I dip the cups into the night, and lift the dipper to my lips, and drink.

Constellations are make-believe, I know, imaginary renditions of the night, but what wonderful fancies! The stars are real, but not the lines that join them. But then, the stars themselves are not always real, and we see the light from suns long dead. It doesn't matter. The imaginary is no less real to me, to this child lying on her back across the bow of the *Michaela*, than anything else.

Chapter 54

After the storm, Pear did not take the *Michaela* into the water again. The boat sat beside the shed like a monument. Deposited on the side lawn on orders from Nana.

She had the notion that she'd pot the boat with annuals, red and white splashes, something easy to grow and overflowing, she said. Bought big bags of soil, cow manure, and other gardener's delights, had the groundskeeper pile them beside the boat, and then ten flats of impatiens. A strange flower for Nana to pick, I remember wondering, for impatience rules my body, not hers, and a strange thing for her to want to do, plant the boat. Maybe if the *Michaela* were grounded, really grounded, earth and flowers and roots, she thinks, we wouldn't be subjected to storm again.

But I'll have none of it, none of boat that is potted plant, none of her impatiens. I kick and scream and bite, so that my teeth leave indentations on Nana's skin, draw blood through her canvas garden gloves. I sit myself in the *Michaela*, refuse to let her plant it.

When she finally stops trying to drag me off the *Michaela*, trying to toss me overboard, she orders the Aunties and the groundskeepers not to speak to me, to make me sit alone, without food and drink and book. *We'll see how long it'll take her to abandon ship,* Nana says, hands on her hips. Little does she know.

I sit in the *Michaela* all through the day. Then lie in the *Michaela,* lifejacket under my head as pillow. Stay put there through lunch, tea, dinner. Watch the star closest to Earth travel the sky, journey from sunrise to sunset.

Mildred is Nana's lookout, peers out the window. The Aunties find chores to do outside the house, wash and shine the windows, beat the carpet over the railing of the porch, pin clothes to the clothesline, *wind drying them so they'll smell fresher,* they say to each other in loud voices in case Nana is listening.

The Aunties edge closer and closer to the boat, slip me things in clever ways so Nana and Mildred don't know what they're doing. Leave me a chocolate bar, and a banana, and a juice box on the gunwale, or other boat places.

Sometimes they work in unison, one distracting Mildred while the other makes the drop. I get a hat to block the midday sun, and later in the evening, a blanket to block the cold. I stay there all night, the stars helping me conquer the dark, and I'm not afraid, not too much, anyway. The light in the kitchen never goes off, and I can see the outline of Nana inside, and she sips tea, and waits for the abandonment. The jumping of ship.

The next morning, Pear picks me up in his arms out of the boat, carries me with blanket still wrapped around my body to the house, and climbs the winding stairs, carries me down the long hallway to my room, puts me to bed.

Nana comes into the room, and sighs.

She feels my head to see if I've caught a fever, and does not mention ever again the planting of the *Michaela.*

*****

Lily and I lie on our backs across the bow of the *Michaela,* under the night sky. We are no longer children. It has been four years since Dog died, and still we carry grief in our hearts, carry each other in our hearts. Lily's head fits into the crook of my neck

like a puzzle piece, her raven hair black against my pale skin.
I stretch out my arm, straight as arrow. This is what I tell her:
Follow the line of my arm to fingertip, and then beyond. Extend
the imaginary line from fingertip into night sky. Trace the path
from shoulder to star. Look at where I point, and there is Vega.
See how the lesser stars pale next to it, how they're eclipsed.

And there, north of Vega. Follow my finger upward,
trace the line to the tip of the handle of the Little Dipper, and
you'll touch Polaris. The Pole Star. It's a hot blue star, two
thousand times more brilliant than our own sun. Polaris is a
traveller's beacon, a lighthouse for celestial sailors.

Navigatoria, another name for Polaris, the Navigator's
Star. It signals north. Marks the North Celestial Pole, the center
around which all of the stars in the Northern Hemisphere
circulate. But that, too, is illusion, for it's the Earth's rotation that
gives the sense of the star's slow dance, the sky a ballroom.

We have only to look to the night sky to see Dog, to
remember him, to remember each other. Shift your view
southward, connect the stars. Draw Canis Major with your
fingertips, the Larger Dog, and there is Sirius, the Dog Star, the
brightest star in the sky. Its name is derived from the ancient
Greek; it means scorching, searing.

Does it scorch your fingertips? Sear your heart?
Our love?

Chapter 55

My man of silence. I imagine your leaving. How you left me that night on the hill, or was it early dawn? How you stole away, extricated yourself from the sleeping bag, extricated yourself from me. Lifted away my arm, lifted it off your body, laid it carefully down. Froze your position in a crouch when I stirred. Your black dog whining at your heels, eager to play now that you are up, and you shush him, *quiet now, don't wake Michaela.* You slowly stand. Search out your shoes, one under the edge of the sleeping bag, the other in the knot of wildflowers growing on the hillside where we fucked.

You take your canvas bag, sling it over your shoulder, a few joints, a few smokes, a bit of change, leave the sleeping bag. Sleeping bags are easily replaced. So are girls. You pause at my knapsack. Think about dumping it over, shuffling through my things, pocketing anything of value. But you don't, and perhaps that is a sign of weakness, passing by an opportunity.

You and your black dog wind your way down the hill, follow the coiling path, the stars diminishing against the early morning sky. How like a gypsy. Gone without a trace, not even a depression of your body left in the sleeping bag where you lay next to me.

I look to see what you've ripped off. Don't know which makes me angrier, that I've been scammed, your stealing from me, or that I've been twice scammed, a cheap trick on a hilltop. Didn't cost you a cent, and you're gone before the stars.

I shake the bag, turn it upside down, dump my belongings on the ground. Socks, makeup, earrings, wallet, flashlight, a few condoms still in the package, a bottle of Aspirin, a pack of cigarettes, a joint, a Kleenex, my knife, a roll of bills wrapped up in an elastic band, clothes, underwear. Throw them about so that they scatter across the ground. I can't find the box that carries my home. Holds it like the dot on the map holds a city, holds the picture of the gypsy woman. The other possessions in the small box, the silver dollar, seashell, silver fountain pen. I can live without them. But not the gypsy woman.

I rifle through my clothes. Then I feel it, wrapped in Thomas's flannel shirt, a hard lump in the center. Peel away the shirt. Reveal the box. It's all there, even her. I start to cry. Shove my belongings into the knapsack, shove in the wad of cash, shove in the box. Follow your path down the side of the hill.

*****

Rom leave *patrin* when they pull up camp.

Leave deliberate signs that point the other gypsies in the direction of their travel. The slice of a knife in the trunk of the tree, a notch in a dried bone, twigs bundled together and left at the side of the road, a pile of rocks, branches snapped or bent in a certain way.

The band - loosely travelling together, paths crisscrossing - look for the *patrin*. Look for the signs that *gadjo* wouldn't notice, and if they do, wouldn't know how to read, so intent upon their own alphabet. And if they do notice, then they're afraid, read the *patrin* as gypsy curse.

I watch the ground for signs of you. A blade of grass, a wildflower growing at the side of the path, bent over, pressed to the ground where you have stepped, a cigarette butt, a candy wrapper.

I see nothing, although a few times, I spot a paw print pressed into the dirt. It's a partial print, and I think it must be your dog, although it could be another. And then I catch the flash of the wire copper. The wire is twisted into the shape of a small fish. The fish lies at the edge of the path like an arrowhead. I pick it up, hold it in my palm. Turn it over. Examine it.

The workmanship is fine, done with quick care, not fussed over, but fussed enough. The thicker wire has been flattened to form the body of the fish. The thinner wire loops around the body to form the scales, the tail fins, eye.

There's a tiny loop at the tip to hang the charm from a necklace. I thread it through my gold chain, wear the copper fish with the other trinkets and beads that already hang about my neck. And then I search you out.

Look for the *patrin*.

Chapter 56

At first, you space the signs far apart.

Leave them at the fork of the path, the sidewalk, in the gutter at the side of the road. *Go this way, Michaela.*

You let me know that you haven't run away, if I'm smart enough to see the signs, and if not, if I don't notice them, then you have run away, made good your escape.

When I catch the pattern, see the trail you've left, like breadcrumbs leading out of the woods, I'm amused. You leave the signs in unusual places. I untie the copper fish dangling from the young maple tree, sun catching the copper so the fish glints among the green leaves. Add it to my necklace.

I reach the point where the trail is new, and the path we travelled the night before ends. The *patrin* point me in a different direction, and I must read their intention, read them as map. Read *your* intention, read *you* as map.

I grow alert, and then exhilarated, searching out the copper fish. The *patrin* lead me through the downtown core. I find the seventh copper fish lying on the window ledge of a street level shop, and I laugh aloud, because the store sells chic lingerie. I see myself dressed in such silly finery, silk and hand-stitched lace, and then I imagine you in them, and the thought is even funnier, although easier to believe.

The streets are just now waking up, like a child stretching and rubbing his eyes, hair tousled and pajamas wrinkled. It's Sunday, and so the day wakes slowly, sips its coffee rather than gulping it down. There are a few cars, and fewer pedestrians. A street kid picks through the garbage - a street urchin, a street entrepreneur, take your pick. He looks for bottles. Not enough bottles, then the begging begins, the cajoling, threatening, stealing. It's hard work, living on the street.

Even dying on the street takes effort. Lying in an alley until there's nothing more for anyone to take from you. Nothing left and you don't care to live, but you do anyway, because it's harder to die than you thought. So you just pick yourself up, and go on your way again.

*****

The eighth copper fish is pinned to a telephone pole.

The pole is covered with staples and little bits of paper, artifacts of fringe festivals and street performers and underground concerts and bar bands, layers of advertising and street life. It's a cultural excavation. The *patrin* points to a poster that is fresh, a street sale of art by local artisans - today, at the Garden Park in the center of the city.

It's only a short walk to you now. The artisans are gathering, each looking for the most advantageous spot to outsell their rivals. They pretend to be friendly, the artist's spirit of camaraderie, but it's a lie. Their livelihood depends upon the sale. They're cutthroats in disguise.

I look for you. You should stand out among them, your red hair, dark skin, your brow and lip piercing, your black dog. And there you are. Pinning copper art to plain brown cardboard, leaning the cardboard against the wrought iron fence. It's part of the attraction, this simplicity. Your work catches glints of the sun. The bits of dangling jewellery, earrings and necklaces and bracelets and hair clips, glass worked through them, other scrap materials, buttons and faux pearls, even tiny nuts and bolts and washers.

Already you gather onlookers. You smile at them and they fall in love with you. It's a sweet seduction, and they're happy to be seduced. I move closer. Stand by a tree. Listen. You talk about your work, life as an artist. It's all so bohemian, you charm a transaction. Goods and money change hands. You spot me leaning against the tree. There's mischief in your eyes. Delight too, although maybe I imagine it. You come over, and now I've been seduced. You kiss me, and I kiss you back, put my tongue into your mouth, nibble your lip, even though you left me on the hill, left without word of your leaving.

You wear a copper fish around your neck, the same design that hangs eight times around mine. But this final fish is intricate. Its scales, its fins filigree. You slip the charm (the perfect word) from the thin black cord, hand it to me, and I put it around my neck, gypsy curse, gypsy spell, set in motion.

Chapter 57

Nana hides the letters.

Even a child would notice her clumsy efforts, especially a child. Deception is an unusual act for Nana. She's so transparent, out in the open. It's her nature. She says what she thinks, and usually it's brusque, sharp words that don't hold back.

Nana doesn't know how to lie. She has no practice at it. Lying, like anything else, takes practice. It's an acquired skill, although some of us come more naturally to it than others. Learn it on the knee of our parents, as natural as rocking.

Nana watches from the window, pretends to look out casually, the poorly executed deception. Lifts the corner of the soft white curtains in the kitchen, peeks out at the stone curved road in front of the manor. Starts her peeking a half-hour earlier than the mail delivery is expected, and then, an hour earlier. Lets go of the curtain, so that it flutters back into place, the breeze from the open window ruffling it gently.

Nana's nervous. I watch her with curiosity and amusement. For once, she doesn't scold me about homework left undone, or the "inappropriateness" of my clothes for school. She uses words like that, inappropriateness. She needs a translator, someone to put her words into plain language. Even Pear, with his bastardized English, his funny mixture of French into the English, is clearer in what he means.

On a few rare occasions, when her anger boils over, Nana lets down her proper English reserve. Spits out words that, once said, make her angry that she has said them, and then she blames me for making her talk that way. *You look like a slut, Michaela,* she shouts one night as I go out the door, and another time, when she's angry about a missed curfew, *You have the mouth of a truck driver.*

Not a truck driver, I tell her. The mouth of a gypsy.

Gypsy my eye, she says, and she gets angrier when I tell her it has nothing to do with her eye, nothing to do with *her* at all. I'm not her flesh and blood.

Right now, she flitters through household tasks. Opens the dishwasher, puts away a dish or two, shuts the door, the remainder of the dishes left inside. She lifts up the edge of the curtain, peers outside again as if she has forgotten that she looked just five minutes ago. She waters the Christmas cactus twice and the azalea not at all, doesn't talk to the plants, forgets to profess her love to them. Doesn't pluck off the dead leaves, trim back the overgrowth, feed them plant food, deadhead the flowers, churn the earth to aerate their roots. Doesn't repot them, plants spilling out of their containers, withering from this un-Nana-like lack of attention.

The mailbox sits dead center on a pole at the edge of the road that runs past the house. Since Nana's manor is in the country, the mail is delivered by car. Like clockwork, the mailman pulls to a stop alongside the mailbox, his car kicking up stones and dust. Sometimes, the car doesn't stop at all. The mailman opens the box, throws in the bundle while still on the move, missing his target. The mail scatters into the ditch, and the car roars to the next mailbox, kicking up dust, disappearing off down the road.

Nana no longer sends me to get the mail, my chore for years. Won't even let the Aunties, but goes herself. Hurries out as soon as the mailman's car appears. I've watched her from my bedroom window, watched her scurry through the courtyard in her no-nonsense way, such tiny quick steps. Even watched her climb into the ditch, scour through the brush for offending pieces of mail, bits of the long dry grass sticking to her skirt and nylons.

She flips through the mail, fans it quickly, and then censors pieces. When she gets into the house, she goes straight to her room. Hides the letters there, but I resolve to find them soon enough. It'll just take patience. I can be patient when it suits me.

What could unsettle Nana in such a way? Nana, the-flappable?

The letters arrive like homing pigeons.

After a summer of letters, the phone calls start.

Nana carries the phone around in her pocket, wears the same cardigan sweater each day with the big pockets at the side, pockets big enough to carry the receiver with her.

The phone doesn't complete a full ring before Nana's picked it up, speaks in low tones, conversation never more than a minute, and then hangs up the receiver. She answers the ring before anyone else can answer, before *me* in particular. I let her. I have no urge to speak to the caller. By now, I've figured out who it is. The Prodigal Son. The Prodigal Father.

"I won't talk to him," I tell Nana.

"You won't speak to whom?" she says.

Nana lifts the curtain, peers out the window, watches for the mailman again.

"You can't make me," I say.

It's a stupid thing to say, in hindsight. It's been years since Nana has been able to make me do anything. And Pear, well Pear never really tried to make me do anything. Not since I was a child, and he tried to explain the relationship between the man in the photo and me. Père and pear.

Nana sighs. She turns away from the window, looks at my clothes, the low-cut top, the butt-short skirt, the high-heels, the pierced eyebrow, sighs again.

"To whom, Michaela? To whom do you think I would try to make you talk?"

"The no-good bum," I tell her. "Good for nothing and

hard on food."

"I don't know whom you mean," Nana says, staring through her Christmas cactus, as if it's not there.

"Don't play naïve with me," I say. "You know who I mean. The single black dot of ink against the flat pen line of the horizon."

Nana still pretends not to know, and I feel the quickening step of rage in my body.

"Your *son*. Michael," I yell. "The pale blond guy that stares down from the fucking pedestal of the mantelpiece. No picture of my mother, just *him*."

The rage now runs through me. My body thinks to storm out of the kitchen. But bodies don't really think, they act. And for once, I don't do what my body wants. I stay. I won't let Nana off the hook so easily by leaving.

Nana ignores my profanity. It's unusual that she does that, my swearing a constant sore point between us. "Of course I can't make you talk to him," she says.

I think she's done. I gloat. I've won. A concession from her. I stand up to leave, grab breakfast on the way out, a handful of cookies, but she is not done yet.

"Of course I can't make you talk to him," she repeats. "Not unless you're thinking of running away again."

I smirk. I run away every night. Come back when I please. I suppose that technically isn't running away anymore, but simply coming and going. Last place I'd go is to see *him*.

I move to leave. But Nana still isn't done. She has more to say. "You'd need a psychic. Better yet, a medium."

It's a strange comment. I puzzle over her words. I decide her son is dead to her. That she has disowned him, like I have. That he might as well be six feet under to both of us.

We have something in common, Nana and me. Our dead. I'm nice to her for awhile, don't swear so much around the house, tone down my clothes, leave out the lip ring, come home at night only an hour or two past curfew, even water her plants. Pull off the dead leaves, repot the plants with the roots growing out the drainage hole. Even try to be creative, put dirt in a red stiletto shoe, and plant a rooted ivy slip in it, pressing the earth firmly around the stem with my fingertips.

In this moment, Nana checks the window again, lifts the corner of the soft white curtain. And right now, instead of storming out of the door, the sound ricocheting behind me like a string of bullets, I walk across the linoleum floor to where she stands, bend over (for I am now much taller than Nana), and softly kiss her cheek. It was Nana who taught me to read, and if I love Pear for the wheelbarrow and boat, then I love Nana for the books and maps, if nothing more.

She smiles a sliver at the unexpected kiss, and then I leave, shutting the door quietly behind me.

Chapter 58

"Marry me," Thomas says.

Thomas is sincere. He's incapable of the opposite. He doesn't know how to lie, how to twist the tale. It's not in his nature. He's a stranger to story, the distance travelled between the truth and untruth. With Thomas, what you see is what you get.

"Go back to sleep," I tell him.

It's the third time he has asked this week.

I pull the blanket over my head, block out Thomas's words. Block out his insistence, his claim of what is love.

Marriage is the only outcome he can imagine. This isn't love, Thomas's confusion and my rooted-ness. Holy matrimony, what's so holy about it? He mistakes much for love that isn't.

We've lived as man and wife, so man and wife we must become. He's incapable of imagining any other way, any other road. For Thomas there is no journey, just the place. His understanding of commitment keeps him rooted. Mine keeps me moving.

The room is hot. There's no thermostat, and we can't regulate the temperature, dependent upon the landlord. Spring has come swiftly, ignoring the calendars. The furnace cranks out heat. I kick off the blanket, it's too hot for blankets. The air is dry, and I lick my lips. The skin is cracked, and my head pounds. Maybe I'm ill. More likely, I'm dehydrated, hung over from the wine. Maybe it is the smell of cigarettes. Thomas has started smoking, one after another. The ashtray is full of butts.

Thomas touches my thigh. He wants to make love again. I pull myself out of the bed, walk to the refrigerator, pop ice cubes from the tray so they scatter across the counter. Pick one up between my fingers, press it against my lips. It alleviates my discomfort, but not fully. I'm restless, edgy.

"You're not at school," I say.

It's a stupid statement. It's obvious he isn't at the seminary. He's in bed naked. Thomas's penis can't even lie, can't hide his intent. It's seminal, but not seminary. Maybe I just want to pick a fight.

I've stopped asking him questions, stopped asking if he's going to classes, and then why he isn't. I *know* why. He confuses me with theology. Confuses me with ideas. Confuses me with the seminary. Confuses me with all those things that he is, those things at the center of his being, those things that if he splits the wood, are there. I am not them. Neither are my fingers on his body, nor my fingers on mind. Neither is the wine, or the candles like stars.

I reach to the floor, scoop up clothes. I don't have to reach far; they're everywhere. I throw a handful at Thomas. He catches a flannel shirt, pulls it on reluctantly, shoves an arm through a sleeve, then another. Buttons up the front so that the two sides don't match, one part dangling longer than the other, picks up socks, tugs them on. They don't match either. His toes push through wool.

"Mary, I want you for my wife," Thomas says.

Fourth time this week.

"I won't marry you, Thomas," I say. "Priests can't have wives, for God's sake."

He takes my hand, stands in front of me, dressed in flannel shirt and socks. His legs are bare, thighs skinny, knees big. There's something sweet about him.

I don't want sweet.

He clasps my fingers as if to let go would mean to lose me. There's desperation in the act, and I pull slightly away, test the grip. He won't let go.

"Mary," he says.

"*Michaela*," I counter silently.

Split the wood and I am there.

Then Thomas pauses, and I can see him thinking, to tell me or not to tell me, and then he says it, says what is on his mind besides our marriage.

"I'm leaving the seminary," he says. "I'm giving up the idea of being a priest."

Idea of being a priest.

Thomas, for you it's all about ideas. Nothing else. You need ideas as deeply as I need to leave. You are scholar. But I don't say this to him. He won't understand, will only protest.

Then Thomas drops to one knee. It's so silly, so old-fashioned, so *Thomas*, that I don't even laugh. I dare not laugh, because it would hurt him. But I don't know how to escape hurting him, and if I could escape, escape this room, escape this moment, escape this road, I would.

"Be my wife," Thomas says. "It is all that I want."

"You don't know what you-" I start to say, and then I stop, leave my sentence where it is, don't finish it.

"Yes, Thomas," I tell him. "I'll marry you."

Chapter 59

If it were weather, then leaving is a summer storm. You feel it in the air before it happens.

The days lie behind you in an endless stretch of heat and non-movement, where the weather simply sits there, the sun shining and the sky flawless blue, the birds chirping and raising their young, their first, second, third brood. The flowers in the garden over-bloom, well rooted by now and profuse in their gratitude. It's what they know, what they understand, so who can fault them?

Electric fans are placed strategically to move air around the room, but it's not the same as a gust of wind. People drink lemonade or beer or iced cappuccino, whatever their preference, as long as it's cold. The old people on the street, the winos and the lonely, lie on the park benches, and you think they're dead. You nudge them, and they grunt, shift position, and you leave them to sleep off the heat.

The weather sits there, like a stagnant pool of water. But what do you nudge? You just wait. Wait it out. The birds, the flowers, the flawless blue sky.

The summer storm is never gentle. The change in weather is swift when it comes. It swoops, rages into hurricane winds, tropical and hot. Trees bend and then splash back again. Snap back, the tops of the trees tossed like a small boat in a gale. The wind carries rain in it, so that the atmosphere is saturated. You can feel rain against your body, impending and thick.

If you're vigilant, you feel the storm before it breaks. It's your storm watch, this edginess in the air, this edginess in you. If you're vigilant, you know the signs, pack your bag and leave. Be well on your way before it hits.

*****

Leaving is much like the end of journeys, the arc of story before it slips upward into the next story.

Sometimes it is dramatic. Swoops, as sudden as adrenaline. Other times the leaving is a gentle slope. Builds slowly, and you see the signs along the road, and you try to ignore them, but there they are, and you know you're going, and the real question is when.

There's no gentle way to say *I love you*, to travel body, and then be gone in the morning, no note, no words, no story to explain your absence, no *patrin*. But sometimes it's the only way, as much an act of love as any other.

Chapter 60

I dream Lily.

We're in a small dark room.

The sensation of room is not just visual. It's tactile. I mean my words, choose them well. The room *feels* thick and luxurious and safe, and just not as metaphor. It touches me. This dream is really about touch, I come to realize as I speak it aloud. Put it into words. Sometimes it takes the telling to know such things.

Lily kneels at the end of the sofa. I reach for her face. It's dark, and I don't know from sight that it's her. I know from touch. I *feel* her face in my sleep, run my fingers along it, feel her cheeks beneath my fingers. And in some strange way, I make her real through my touch, make us both real. I put my hands beneath her shirt, cup her breasts. She takes on substance, becomes substantial. This *happens* in the dream, this fleshing out of her. I feel it.

A young girl sits in the corner. She has long beige hair. An old woman sits in the other corner. She, too, has long beige hair. I don't know who they are, nor why they're here, but they don't feel like intruders. They belong, as much as Lily and me belong, but that is all I can tell you, all I know. A dream is like story. Who can explain it? I linger in the dream. Feel its weight beneath my fingers.

Chapter 61

After Lily's family picks up and moves a whole world away, takes her with them, I still run away to the church, run away in the dead of night. The boys are not as much fun as Lily, but they have their own charm, and their own peculiarities. I know only my own body for comparison, and the lips of Lily. Lily's lips are soft, and the boy's lips are rough, but rough can be intriguing, too.

My chest is growing breasts. Tiny things, but breasts nonetheless. Pubic hair is sprouting from me, spindly pale pubic hair. So pale and spindly that when I look in the mirror, stand there naked, I hardly see hair at all, unless I peer closely. Still, my skin camouflages the hair so well that there appears to be no pussy at all, no bushy kitty-cat curled up asleep in my lap.

Hair grows from my armpits, and from my legs. But unlike the other girls my age, and some girls even younger, I don't have to shave every day to hide it. Like the pussy-hair, this hair also blends with my pale skin. Skin the colour of cheese, the colour of the moon, the colour of barn straw, hair like corn silk. I'm a late-bloomer to use a phrase from Nana's lexicon, but who wants to be known as a flower. Maybe others, the Rosemarys, and even the Lilies of the world, but not me. The other girls have bigger breasts, and have them much sooner. They've curves in their hips where I've straight lines.

At first I'm angry with these girls, throw their schoolbooks into the garbage when they aren't looking, and sometimes when they are looking. Pull their hair, kick their shins, blacken their eyes, get expelled from school for violence and other inappropriate behaviour. It's a catchall, made the expelling easier for the school. They named me, and my name was Inappropriate. Then I'm angry with myself for being so unlike my mother, so unlike Lily. I imagine their curves, and their gypsy hair, thick and black, a longhaired cat. I curse my genes and then take back the curse, for it's not the genes that are to blame, but the curse itself.

But none of this really matters to the boys, as long as I put out, and so they meet me at the church in the middle of the night. And so it goes, until one night, Nana comes too. Follows me from home, catches me under the communion rail with my blouse up, and my pants down. She doesn't understand that I'm searching for love and the surge it brings to the heart. I try on different boys for size, to see if they fit, but none do. I don't feel that surge again, love like adrenaline, until I find you, hair aflame, crouched on the street, wrapped in a sleeping bag. And a dog, too, wrapped up with you. It's enough to make me believe in fate.

I find orgasms aplenty in the church, but that's just skilful manipulation. Even the most dim-witted and dim-fingered among the boys could be taught to manipulate with guidance. I'm not stupid enough to mistake love for titillation, multiple or otherwise. It's in the throes of one such search that Nana's voice breaks through the passion of the moment. A short moment at that, for the boy is new to this game, and I must coach him along, take his hand and put it where it should go, even move it for him. He is wide-eyed, stares at me in shock and fear, a deer in the lights of a car.

"Close your eyes," I order, the dominatrix.

He closes his eyes.

"Michaela!"

I don't recognize Nana's voice, unexpected as it is. I look at the boy in surprise. He doesn't have it in him, to shout my name with such a force.

"Michaela!"

Nana stands on the other side of the altar rail. She can't step over the boundary into the altar space of God. She's religious. And rooted.

"Pull up your pants!" she says.

I comply, pull up my pants. The boy turns red from ear to ear, and scampers ass up, hides behind the altar cloth.

"You are *so young*, Michaela, just fifteen, and look at you!"

Nana's voice is tight. She constrains herself, like a plant that is root-bound. She wants to burst the pot, but she won't.

"Nadja and Nicu were *married* at thirteen," I tell her in my defense, not that I believe I need to defend my actions.

"Who is Nicu?" Nana says.

But it's the next question that sends my adrenaline pumping. She speaks the words that I can't forgive.

"Who is Nadja?" Nana says.

"My mother," I scream.

"Here's truth for certain," Nana says. "You're just like your mother, Michaela."

My anger softens. It's the first time I have heard Nana refer to my mother, and then to say I'm just like her.

"She was a slut, too," Nana adds.

The words hang there between us. Nana breathes in deeply, wants to breathe the words back into herself.

But she can't, words don't work that way, and neither do stories. You can't take them back. They have a life of their own.

Chapter 62

I traced Nadja's travels many times on Nana's atlas, the *At Last! At Last!*

Each time the journey was different, the route circuitous, and rambling, but Nadja always eventually reached the Atlantic Ocean. Through Romania, a side trip to Bulgaria, through imaginary Yugoslavia, gone the way of Czechoslovakia, turning northward, travelling beneath the shadow of the Carpathian Mountains, slipping southward again, through Hungary, Austria, into Germany, into France. And now, *at last,* I come to the part in the journey where the circle meets, like the lines of latitude on the globe.

The *gadjo* traveller returns home at the end of the journey like the cows to the barn at the end of the day. Arrival and departure stamped on their tickets, and so it must be. There are things to do, and cameras to unload, and film to develop, and photographs to paste into albums. Captions to devise, pithy and witty, and printed underneath in neat block letters. Then underneath again, date and time, who and with whom. Exact destinations and exact locations. Facts recorded diligently for the future, for how many photos get stuffed into shoeboxes and shoved into closets, and then one day, no one recognizes the faces, nor can name the journeys.

But the gypsy doesn't care.

The journey is her home, and Rom is a state of mind. She doesn't need a record outside of herself, and carries the record with her. But as any true Traveller knows, the road never ends, and neither does the tale. There are story arcs, and journey arcs, dips and valleys, and twists and turns that give the illusion of endings, of beginnings.

*****

I leave the boy quaking at the altar. I've no respect for a boy who quakes, altar or not. He's not worthy of my attention, and I spit in his direction, curse him before I leave. I must do something, and it's the least of responses for the moment. If he were worthier, I might have beat him senseless. Felt my fists against his flesh and bone, such was my anger.

I don't go back to the manor, as Nana orders. I wander the streets, drink them in. I know it's the last time I'll be here, and take my fill.

When I reach the edge of the town, I keep walking. Walk the road where I first met Lily, walk its length. The distance is so short now. How does that happen? Distances shrink? What we know to be true changes on us like that?

I follow the path through the meadow to the old barn where Dog and I hid, told stories to each other. The barn has fallen into itself, a large pile of rotting wood. I circumambulate the wood, like it is Mecca, the Dome of the Rock, and I, a holy traveller. Finally, I stop my circumambulating, and then it's dawn. The sky is rose-pink, and I don't sentimentalize it. Sentimentality makes the leaving more difficult and the adrenaline less effective. I channel my anger to resolve. I'm leaving.

I finally return to the manor. Don't tiptoe. Barge. Let the stairs creak loudly and the doors bang. I'm still angry at Nana, even hours after she has followed me to the church. There's no sense keeping quiet. I'm not sneaking back into the house. I've made up my mind. I don't need to hide the truth.

What can Nana do?

She can't keep me here forever. I can pick the locks, open the windows, jump out if I wish, fly to the ground, if Mildred's truths are true, and I suppose they're as true as any other. Like all of us, she twists her own stories.

I grab some clothes, a few hundred dollars I've stashed under my mattress, some possessions - a page ripped from a book, a seashell, a silver dollar. I'm almost ready. Almost. There's still the matter of the letters.

I know where Nana keeps them.

The hiding place is no longer a secret, although she thinks it is. She's so predictable, I tell myself.

But I'm wrong. Not about the hiding place, but about Nana. She isn't predictable. I didn't predict it. The story she would tell me.

I've watched her for months now from my window. Watched her hurry to the mailbox, those quick little steps, as if she's afraid to break out into a run. Watched her sift through the mail, a quick once-through, scanning the envelopes, as if she fans a deck of cards. Never could I tell which day a letter might arrive, which day Nana would pull out an envelope, tuck it into her sweater pocket, hurry into the house, place the rest of the mail in a bundle on the hallway table, as if nothing was askew.

Then I'd hear Nana's feet on the steps, up the long staircase, stairs creaking loudly in that way they always do when you try to be quiet. When the creaking had stopped, I knew that Nana had turned down the hallway, the carpet cushioning her feet. I'd hear the door to her room push open, the hinges squeaking, and then her dresser drawer open. There's a noise to everything, if you listen. It's a useful skill.

I stride into her room, so full of confidence and adrenaline, both feeding off each other. Pull open Nana's underwear drawer where she stores her secrets.

I'm always surprised anew by the fact that she wears silk underwear. And not black. Pastel shades, baby blue and soft pink and even melon orange. It's so unlike her.

When I was a child, I would play under the clothesline

and Nana's underwear would billow above me like pretty silk sails. I would pretend I was a ship in a flotilla. Not a sailor, but the ship itself, the mode of transportation of my own desire. I'd play for hours, take myself away, independent of the others. I didn't need them, for I could carry myself to distant ports, sail off one page into the next one. Travel to all the dots of the maps.

At the bottom of Nana's underwear drawer, as I knew they would be, are the letters. She has bundled them with an elastic band.

"Michaela," a voice says softly.

Nana stands in the shadows. The curtains are closed, and the room is dark. My eyes make out her line, then fill in shape and detail. She's dressed in the clothes she wore last night, her hair is unkempt. She hasn't slept.

Pear's French Canadian snores arise from the bedroom down the hall. It has just been another night for him - he is accustomed to my running away.

"You had only to ask," Nana says. "I would have shown you the letters. There's no need to rifle through my drawers like a common-"

She stops herself. I finish the sentence for her.

"Thief," I say. "Thief *and* slut."

I lift the bundle out of her drawer, hold the letters in my hands.

"Michaela," Nana says. "Please, wait. Come, let's go down into the kitchen and have tea, we can discuss this-"

How like the English to want to negotiate treaties over tea. But I've no intention of surrendering the letters to Nana, nor surrendering myself.

I read the name on the top envelope.

It's addressed to me. *Michaela.*

I turn the envelope over. Read the return address. Don't recognize the sender's name.

A woman's name.

I had expected another. The dot on the horizon, prodigal son, prodigal father repents and comes home to make amends. I'm caught off-guard.

"Who's this?"

Nana sighs. It's resignation. That point in the journey where there's no more choice, no more crossroads, *shall I go this way or that way*. She drops her arms to her sides. She seems smaller. There are wrinkles in her face, and her skin is grey, but I'm angry. I don't want to see her aging or her sadness.

"Who's the common thief now, Nana, whose letters have you kept from me?"

I feel the rising tide of adrenaline, and it's familiar, even soothing in its fierceness. I recognize the sensation. I hear the crashing of the trees, the howling of the wind, but it's not the wind. It's my own blood roaring through my heart.

"We tried to tell you, Michaela. When you were a child. But you'd stamp your feet, and cry hysterically, and run away. You were always running away."

It's the wrong choice of tense. She knows that, the knapsack on the floor by the door. There's no past tense in what I'm doing.

"Do you think it was easy for us to bury Michael twice? Never to speak of him, for fear of what you'd do? Jump out a window again?"

Nana's voice has gained belligerence.

Her words make no sense, and I don't care for explanation, such is my anger, my adrenaline.

"Who wrote these letters?" I demand.

I hold Nana by the wrist, and I know I hurt her. It's not my intention to hurt her, but then, neither is it not, for adrenaline has its own intentions.

We stand like that, and Nana knows I won't let go, not until she tells me, and so she speaks.

"Your mother wrote them," she says.

I drop her wrist. Stare at the top envelope.

The penmanship is strong and smooth and uninterrupted, as if resurrecting the dead needs no other truth or lie than a stroke of a pen.

"Nadja?"

"No, not Nadja," Nana says quietly. "Your real mother."

I shove the envelope into my knapsack and become the dot on the brushstroke of my own horizon. Leave for good. Leave forever.

Chapter 63

I wear your *patrin* like coins around a gypsy's neck and woven through my hair. Have knotted the chain so that the *patrin* lie side by side, nine copper fish.

A woman buys a copper bracelet, money passes hands, and then you return to your art, twist the copper. The day is hot, and my skin is turning red. I sit on the grass beside you. Pull on the thread of story, pull the thread up like stitching tapestry.

"Gypsies from Ireland have red hair," I say. "You're an Irish gypsy, then?"

"If you say so, it must be true," you laugh.

Your dog nudges your hand. You kneel down close to him, put your head into his neck.

The sun is harsh. Your hair catches the rays, flares red with the fire of the sun. The fire of the stars, since the sun is a star. You take my hand in your hand. My hand is white against your dark skin, soaked with sun, soaked with star.

"What kind of gypsy are you, Michaela, fair-haired and fair-skinned?" you ask me.

"You've heard the story," I say. "Split the wood and I am there," I add, quoting *The Gospel of Thomas*.

It's ironic that I come to this place once more.

Quote a book given to me by a *gadjo* to prove my case. It's a fitting tribute that I return to Thomas, in thought and mind, although never again in physical journey. I don't retrace my steps, not for anyone - except perhaps someday for Lily.

Chapter 64

We walk along a riverfront. It's not ocean, I'm not there yet, but I draw closer. And when I do arrive, there will be another ocean to find. It's my nature.

I play the game with you. The game I played with Lily.

"There," I say. "Look. If my mother were alive, if she hadn't died in the rocking chair, she'd be just like *her*."

Three women sit on small stools at the end of the dock, and only one of them can be my mother. They face each other in a triangle, beat drums held between their legs, knees wide apart, like old gypsy women who no longer care what others think, have earned the right to sit this way. They each play their own version of the theme. The drumming is rhythmic, hypnotic like story. Themes run into each other, and over each other, waves of sound, and somehow it all makes sense, comes together, layered and rich in variation.

"Which one is her?" you ask.

Two of the women wear jeans. One has salt-pepper hair, coarse and cropped short. She's too old to be Nadja. The other has hair bleached by the sun, and her skin is too freckled to be Nadja. The third woman, now she could be Nadja.

"The woman in the skirt," I tell you.

She pushes the hem up over her legs so that her knees show, the drum pressed between them. Her hair is dark, pulled back in a ponytail at the nape of her neck. She no longer wears her kerchief back-knotted and covering her head, wears it tied around her ponytail, so that her head is bare. But she still wears gold, thick gold hoops through her ear lobes, and a row of small gold studs up the side of her ear. Her sweater is crimson. Nadja always looked good in red.

"Then let's take a closer look," you say.

We walk to the end of the dock, past the three drumming women. I look at Nadja, and she looks up at me. She smiles, as if there is recognition somewhere, and I smile back, in the same way. Nadja keeps drumming, does not miss a beat, and I would expect no less.

"So that's her?" you say.

"Yes," I answer.

And why not?

Why shouldn't that be her? Dead or alive, she's my story to tell. It's all we have, a story and a road. If I must have a mother, and everyone must, I might as well choose her. And choose her well. And if you do not believe that this is my inheritance, then believe that I stole it, took her story as my own, took it as my rightful birthright.

I unlace my hand from your hand, set my knapsack on the dock, reach into it, find an envelope, wrinkled from the journey. Rip the envelope into a million pieces, let the pieces flutter into the sea like the ashes of the dead.

The pieces swirl on the wind, and then the waves, and it's magic. But then the moment shifts and I remember. Torn envelope, that's all. But of course, that isn't all. It never is.

I tell you the rest of my story, tell it by the beat of the drum that is my mother and the beat of the drum that is my heart. We set the letters to the wind, toss them like confetti, set *her* to the wind, the ashes of my dead swept away on its waves. I find myself crying, and there is the taste of salt in my tears, the taste of the sea, the taste of Lily.

Chapter 65

Petros is rock in New Testament Greek. It's another useless fact I've learned from Thomas's books. I read them more than he does, now that he thinks he'll not be a priest, thinks I'll marry him.

Peter is the rock upon which I build my church.

It's early Christian humour, an attempt at word play, Jesus the joker, the standup comedian. The humour is lost in the translation from New Testament Greek to Modern English. Rocky, or even Rocco, the translators should have said, not Peter. *Rocco is the rock upon which I build my church.*

He could be an amusing guy, that Jesus, a lot funnier than the scribes gave him credit, cloistered monks fiddling with gospel truth, changing it to suit their purposes.

In all my readings cloistered in the apartment, there are only a few Christian truths that remain untouched and worthy of their salt. I've found them in an obscure book unburied from beneath the sand, written by one Thomas, and given to me by another. He's the instrument of my own leaving, poor Thomas. If he only knew.

But it doesn't matter, not really, Peter or Rocky. Peter is not the rock. The Apostle Thomas is the rock upon which to build a church. The apostle with the courage to touch an open wound, to question story. To know that there are lies, and that sometimes, in the lie, lies the truth.

Build your house upon rock, Thomas dear. That's you. I don't want a house, but if I must have one, then let it be a houseboat that floats upon the ocean, an uncharted place where the stars spread thickly above me, and there are no city lights to dim their radiance. Let it be a house I carry on my back, a house of my own making, made of stories, and the open road, and a love that's not an anchor.

Let it be a house without roof, and without walls, and through which the wind always blows, and where I can feel the weather upon my skin - always weather upon my skin - and let the love I find there be the same making as this house.

Chapter 66

The leaving is calm when it comes. No confrontations, no surprises, no sudden raging storm. I don't feel adrenaline in my body, simply pack a bag and go while Thomas sleeps.

I leave no *patrin*. No signs along the road for him to find me, no trail to track me down, to point the direction of my travel at the crossroads. No slips of paper with forwarding address or my true name. No bus schedule to indicate destination, no ticket stubs to show time of departure and place of arrival. Not even footsteps pressed into snow, for the snow is gone, and so am I.

If he looks for me, he looks for Mary. Searches for her face in the crowds jostling to get on the bus, in the faces of new students at the seminary library huddled over their books, in the faces of street kids leaning against archways, hanging out in back alleys. Sees the traces of Mary in a smile, in the slouch of a body, and his breath catches, and maybe it is her, he thinks, but then it is not. Checks the mailbox religiously for a sign, a note saying that she is coming back, a letter of explanation for her leaving. Why she didn't marry him, left him at the altar.

Left him *to* the altar, closer to the truth.

Where I know Thomas will find his way again, to his

house built from rock. But he won't find Mary, and I don't retrace journey.

I'm passerby.

*****

When I left the manor, ran away for the last time, I lived by my wits, some of it scam and some of it not. Picked strawberries in season, picked blueberries in season, picked apples in season, picked locks and pockets in season as best as I could. Sold Christmas trees in parking lots in December, spring bouquets on street corners for Mother's Day in May. Sold magazine subscriptions door-to-door, and chocolate bars in front of the liquor store in support of missing children charities, the only missing child supported, *me*. Stole a squeegee and a bucket and washed car windows at street corners. Sold myself on the street corners when it was necessary. Ripped off the drunks, took their money, and kept my body for myself, and they never knew the difference.

Pick-pocketing is a trade I never mastered; caught with my fingers in pockets that were not my own, my hands were fumbling and clumsy. My feet, now, they are never clumsy. I'm sure-footed and confident. It's a talent I inherit from Nadja, the dancer, the traveller, the quick of foot and the quick of scam - the quick and the dead.

Sometimes, I'd let myself be caught.

Scammed my captors out of a dry place for the night, and food for my belly, and company to share a story or two, and none of it costing me a cent. A jail is almost as coveted a place to sleep as a university library, but not quite. No books to read, no Thomas to amuse my mind, to leave a trail of ideas as sure as breadcrumbs. Since my crime was petty, I'd be released - although it took a day or two for the police to ascertain my age and the social workers to find me a foster home to run away from. I didn't want a home, don't want it now, want only for the ground beneath my feet to be always changing. It's a good curse.

For months after I leave Nana and Pear, I don't see the

truth within the lie. It's hard enough to face the resurrection of a mother after living with her death for the span of a childhood. I've rocked myself in the arms of her dying. When I pick clean the bones of story, it's sound that I remember most clearly. Rocker lapping against the hardwood, waves slapping against a wooden ship, the constancy of the sound the only thing that is certain and true. Even I can't untangle the truth from the lie, and it doesn't matter, for story has its own truth, and it's just as valid as any other. We all need lullabies, and I have mine.

Nadja was a good mother, and she taught me well. I still keep her as my own, still carry the picture of the gypsy woman in the small box in my knapsack, carry her with me in my heart, and on the open road, carry her on my back as my home.

Sometimes, I put the box under my pillow, like I did when I was a child, and she seeps into my dreams, becomes my dreams. She's the only mother I care to know, and the only mother I'll ever know. I make sure of that, leave no *patrin*.

The silver-framed photo on the mantle, the man the colour of the moon, the colour of straw, the colour of cheese, tufts of hair the colour of corn silk. With the resurrection of a birth mother comes the death of a birth father. And if all of this is true, and maybe it's not, then my birth father is the one who rocked me, who died in the rocking chair, and my birth mother is the dot on the horizon, and she is more gypsy than even I imagined.

I'm only now able to glimpse into Nana and Pear's sorrow. Recognize in it the memory of Pear's drooping shoulders, his slow walk, his escape into his garage sales, and his junk.

Nana tending her flowers, tending her grief.

Keeping her sorrow in contained spaces, where it thrived in its own way, the leaves of the spider plant tumbling from the hanger, baby spider plants falling like tears.

Grief spilling from windowsills, from flower boxes, filling the spaces of the manor. She tended his memory.

In that way, we were the same.

Her, with her flowers, her gardens.

I, perched on the window, head cocked, listening to gypsy stories on the wind, tending my own memory.

ACKNOWLEDGEMENTS

The facts within the lie of this fiction are based upon a wonderful book by Isabel Fonseca, *Bury Me Standing, The Gypsies and Their Journey.* Her true account of travelling through Europe and living with the gypsies is captivating, in parts, shocking; and to the act of dreaming up this novel, an inspiration.

I am also indebted to the caravan of writers who meet with me along the open road to share and shape story. My thanks for your help in travelling the twists and turns and detours of this gypsy tale.

And of course, as always, my gratitude to my husband, Bob, and my daughter, Samantha. I love you both deeply, and couldn't have dedicated a lifetime to writing without your love and support.

ABOUT THE AUTHOR

Photo by
Betty Phylactou

Marianne Paul lives in Kitchener, Ontario. Her first novel, *The Shunning*, was published by Moonstone Press in 1994. Her fiction, non-fiction and poems have appeared in publications such as Story House, Vox Feminarum, Canadian Author, Western People and The New Quarterly. She is the recipient of a variety of literary awards including the Kitchener-Waterloo Arts Award for Writing, the Okanagan Fiction Award, the Waterloo Region WRAConteur Award for Poetry (2003 and 2004) and the 2006 Canadian Aid Literary Award.

Literacy is a cause about which Marianne is passionate. She is the author of *Literacy is a Family Affair* and *Let's Play Literacy*, as well as several other books and research projects that deal with the importance of reading.

Marianne's house is full of stories half-done and underway - her husband is also a writer. They belong to an active community of writers who come to their home to share works-in-progress and friendship.

Visit Marianne's website at www.mariannepaul.com.